SULTAN

Shubendra is an avid traveller who explores places that have fallen through the cracks of mainstream history. His primary interest is unravelling the long-forgotten stories of early modern India through field research and by analyzing old military accounts. Shubendra is an expert on the military history of eighteenth- and nineteenth-century India. *Sultan* is his first book.

SULTAN

The Legend of Hyder Ali

SHUBENDRA

PAN

First published 2021 by Pan
an imprint of Pan Macmillan Publishing India Private Limited
707 Kailash Building
26 K. G. Marg, New Delhi 110 001
www.panmacmillan.co.in

Pan Macmillan, The Smithson, 6 Briset St, Farringdon, London EC1M 5NR
Associated companies throughout the world
www.panmacmillan.com

ISBN 978-93-89109-07-8

1 3 5 7 9 8 6 4 2

Typeset in Adobe Garamond Pro by R. Ajith Kumar, New Delhi
Printed and bound in India by
Replika Press Pvt. Ltd.

For Sangeetha

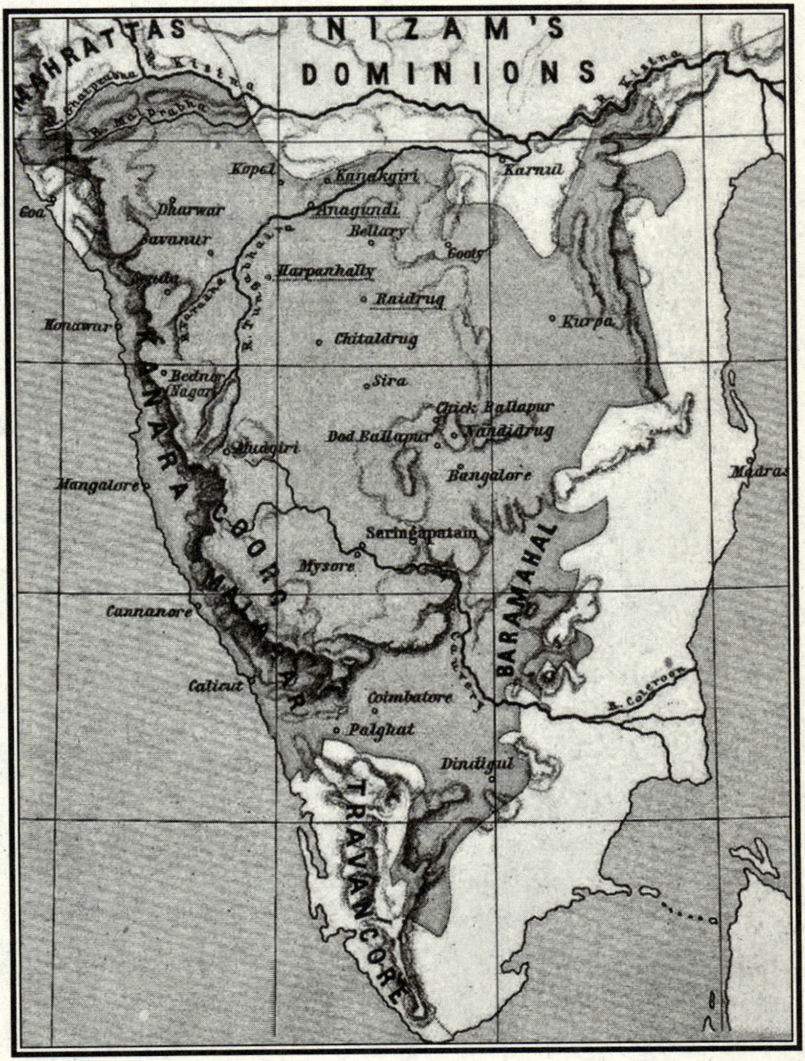

MAHRATTAS
NIZAM'S
DOMINIONS
R. Kistna
Goa
Kopal
Kanakgiri
Karnul
Anagundi
Bellary
Dharwar
Savanur
Gooty
Harpanhally
Raidrug
Honawar
Chitaldrug
Kurpa
Bednor
Nagar
Sira
Chick Ballapur
Dod Ballapur
Nandidrug
Mangalore
Madras
Bangalore
Seringapatam
Mysore
KANARA
COORG
MALABAR
BARAMAHAL
Cannanore
Calicut
Coimbatore
Palghat
Dindigul
TRAVANCORE
R. Coleroon

Cast of Characters

The Mughals

Aurangzeb

Muhammed Azam Shah

Bahadur Shah I

Jalandar Shah

Farrukhsiyar I

Sira

Rasul Khan, Nawab of Sira

Darga Quli Khan, Rasul Khan's father

Fateh Mohammed, General of Sira

Lal Bi, Fateh Mohammed's second wife

Shahbaz, Fateh Mohammed's fourth son

Ramachandra, Fateh Mohammed's astrologer

Hyder, Fateh Mohammed and Lal Bi's son

Hydur Nayaka, Fateh Mohammed's brother

Doddaballapur

Kuli Khan, Rasul Khan's brother and Jagirdar of Doddaballapur

Abbas Khan, Kuli Khan's confidant

Hyderabad

Nizam Asaf Jah, Nizam of Hyderabad

Nasir Jung, Nizam Asaf Jah's son and Nizam after Jah

Muzaffar Jung, Nasir Jung's nephew and pretender to the throne

Salabat Jung, Asaf Jah's second son and Nizam after Muzaffar Jung

Basalat Jung, Salabat Jung's younger brother

Arcot

Saadatullah Khan, Nawab of Arcot

Chanda Sahib, Nawab of Arcot

Wallajah, Nawab of Arcot

Mysore

Devaraja, Diwan of Mysore

Dalwai Nanjaraja, commander-in-chief and brother of Devaraja

Chikka Devaraja Wodeyar, King of Mysore

Krishnaraja Wodeyar, King of Mysore

Chamaraja Wodeyar, Krishnaraja Wodeyar's brother

Nanjaraja Wodeyar, Krishnaraja Wodeyar's first son and king after him

Chamaraja Wodeyar, king after Nanjaraja Wodeyar

Asma, Hyder Ali's first wife

Fatima, Hyder Ali's second wife

Mir Sahib, Fatima's brother

Tipu Mastan Aulia, saint after whom Tipu is named

Tipu, Hyder and Fatima's first son

Karim, their second son

Majeeda, their daughter
Khande Rao, Hyder's accountant
Lutf Ali Beg, Hyder's general
Mohammed Ali, Hyder's general
Shamiayya, Hyder Ali's revenue minister
Lal Mian, Tipu's father-in-law
Burhan-ud-din, Tipu's favourite commander
Purniah, an accountant under Hyder Ali

Poona
Peshwa Madhav Rao
Narayan Rao, Peshwa Madhav Rao's younger brother
Raghunath Rao, Peshwa Madhav Rao's uncle
Trimuk Rao, Maratha general
Morari Rao, Maratha general
Nana Fadnavis, minister leading the revolt against Raghunath Rao
Baarbhai, a Maratha general

The English
Robert Clive
Colonel Smith
Colonel Wood
Colonel Nixon
Colonel Lang
General Hector Munro
Colonel Baillie
Colonel Braithwaite
Governor General Warren Hastings
Eyre Coote, Commander-in-chief of Bengal

Madurai

Trimuk Nayaka, Nayaka of Madurai

Munka Rai, Trimuk Nayaka's wife

Bednur

Rani Viramma

Basappa Nayaka, her late husband

Venkatachala Rao, Diwan of Bednur

Venkatappa, Dalwai of Bednur

Kannur

Ali Raja, chieftain of Kannur

Calicut

The Zamorin

Kumaran Nambiar

Rayadurga

Krishnappa, Palegar of Rayadurga

Chitradurga

Madakari Nayaka, Palegar of Chitradurga

Rangappa and Thimanna, his brothers-in-law

The French

Lally

General Bussy

Kadapa

Hakeem Khan, Nawab of Kadapa

Prologue

AT THE ZENITH OF ITS POWER, MUGHAL EMPEROR Aurangzeb's empire stretched from Kashmir in the north all the way to the southern parts of India. In 1687, in order to efficiently administer the newly conquered regions of South India, Aurangzeb created two *subah*s, or provinces, and named them Hyderabad and Sira. The governors appointed to administer these provinces were to report directly to the emperor. The larger of the two was Hyderabad, which lay to the east and stretched beyond Arcot right down to Thanjavur in the south. The other Mughal province, Sira, lay to the west of Hyderabad and included regions leading up to the Western Ghats.

All the *nayaka*s, *palegar*s and other small rulers within these two provinces were left to rule independently as long as they accepted the suzerainty of the Mughal emperor. Accepting suzerainty meant that these local rulers had to pay a *paishkash*, a tribute in the form of coins minted with the name of the emperor, routed through Mughal governors into the Mughal coffers.

But Aurangzeb's empire, held together only by the force of his will, fell apart after his death in 1707. His successors,

Muhammed Azam Shah, Bahadur Shah I, Jalandar Shah and Farrukhsiyar I, were not as competent as him and could not maintain Mughal authority in hostile territories. They had neither his iron will nor the military skills and political acumen required to hold a vast empire together. Various subordinate kingdoms started gnawing away at the Mughal territories. Soon, all order was lost within the empire. Anarchy ensued.

The Nizam of Hyderabad, Asaf Jah, was the first to declare independence. He managed to keep most of his province together, except for the region of Arcot. He demanded and obtained paishkash from the local chieftains in his province. Only this time, the paishkash remained in Hyderabad rather than reaching the treasury in Delhi. But when the *subahdar*, the governor of Sira, declared independence and demanded paishkash for himself, every ruler and man under him worth his salt now saw themselves as independent as well and refused to pay the annual tribute to the governor or to the Mughal emperor. One such kingdom where citizens defied the law of the land was Mysore.

Mysore was a petty vassal state in the ancient Vijayanagar empire which came into its own in 1673, during the reign of Chikka Devaraja Wodeyar. Wodeyar was a man who chose his battles tactically. He defeated small nayakas and palegars who were no longer of interest to the Mughals and kept expanding his empire little by little until his annexations caught the eye of Aurangzeb.

Wodeyar was a smart man. He didn't want to risk the wrath of the Mughal emperor. As soon as the Mughal ambassadors made their appearance in his court, he pledged his allegiance to the Mughals by paying a significant amount of money as tribute. In return, Aurangzeb recognized him as an important feudatory of the Sira province.

Chikka Devaraja Wodeyar had, in essence, paid the Mughal governors for his freedom to rule and expand his kingdom without interference. With Aurangzeb's death, there was nothing to stop him from declaring independence. But, as fate would have it, he passed away within months after the Mughal emperor's death. His small empire passed on to the hands of his *diwan*, the prime minister, and the *dalwai*, or the chief military general, who promptly refused to pay the annual tribute to their Mughal overlord in Sira.

Meanwhile, in the southwest regions of the Mughal empire, the Marathas seized their chance to assert independence. They had been a fanatical challenge to the Mughals even during the time of Aurangzeb. But Aurangzeb's authority had kept them limited to guerrilla warfare against the numerically superior Mughal army. After his death, however, they emerged as the most aggressive of the challengers to the Mughals, quickly filling the void created by Aurangzeb's successors. They rapidly morphed from a guerrilla army to an imposing conventional military power in the region. Such was the power of the Marathas that unpaid Mughal soldiers started joining their ranks, swelling their numbers. Soon, the Marathas took over the role of imposing order over the smaller rulers in the southern regions of India, without any formal orders from the Mughals. Having lost real control over his southern provinces, the Mughal emperor Farrukhsiyar I issued a *farman*, a royal edict, to the Marathas, that allowed them to collect annual tributes from all the rulers and chieftains in southern India who were not under the Nizam of Hyderabad, in the name of the Mughal emperor. The proceeds would remain in the hands of the Marathas. The Mughals wanted to maintain a semblance of authority over their southern provinces and the Marathas wanted legitimacy to collect revenue from the region. The farman was the perfect solution for both.

This royal edict soon morphed into the *chauth*, an annual tax equal to a fourth of the total revenue earned by the local rulers, which was significantly higher than what the Mughals had collected. Naturally, this led to a lot of discontent amongst the chieftains. But the army of the Marathas was the most fearsome of the land. They offered no space for negotiation and showed no mercy. They would pillage cities and burn villages to the ground until they had received their chauth. They demonstrated this time and again in Gujarat and Khandesh. So, the chieftains grudgingly accepted the increased demands of the Marathas.

Since Mysore was a feudatory of the Mughal province of Sira, the Marathas saw it as their right to collect chauth from here as well. Meanwhile, the Nizam of Hyderabad saw himself as the natural successor of the Mughals in southern India and expected an annual tribute from Mysore as well. That was how, at the start of the eighteenth century, the kingdom of Mysore found itself without a proper ruler and stuck between two seemingly strong forces vying for its riches.

Amidst all this chaos, the English and the French had quietly strengthened their positions on the coasts of India. They had already demonstrated their military and technological superiority by successfully defeating many an Indian chieftain in Bengal and Gujarat. The archaic armies of the local Indian chieftains vastly outnumbered the smaller but nimbler European ones. Yet, they were routinely routed. The Europeans no longer saw themselves as merchants trading in spices, cotton, raw silk and other commodities. They had set their sights on a much bigger prize: a piece of India.

1

1721, Budikote

THE SUMMER OF 1721 WAS UNUSUALLY HOT. FATEH Mohammed was in a pensive mood. Perched on the *masand*, his small throne in his *jagir* of Budikote, he thought about the dark clouds looming over the Mughal province of Sira. As a loyal subject of Sira, the middle-aged general, dusky, with a salt-and-pepper beard, knew it was his duty to protect its new nawab, Rasul Khan, from the impending invasions being mounted by Nizam Asaf Jah of Hyderabad and the Nawab of Arcot, Saadatullah Khan. It was only a question of time before they marched towards Sira. Rasul Khan, unlike his father, Darga Quli Khan, didn't have the stomach to defend Sira, and the great city deserved better. Standing with Rasul Khan would have disastrous consequences, but it was circumstances like these that distinguished a loyalist from an opportunist. Fateh Mohammed had served Sira since the reign of Darga Quli Khan, and the latter had bestowed the jagir of Budikote on him for his loyalty. The late nawab knew that when the call to defend Sira came,

Fateh Mohammed, a man of honour, would be the first to take up arms.

Even as he pondered the fate of Sira, his mind wandered to his own home, and fear crept into his mind. He had not heard anything from the zenana. His wife had gone into labour in the morning and even with the sun setting down over the small fort of Budikote, word from the ladies' quarters was yet to arrive. His first wife had passed away in childbirth. Now, the fear of losing his second wife engulfed him.

Just then, a young girl rushed out of the zenana and into the hall where Fateh Mohammed was ruminating about the future.

'God has been merciful, my lord! The begum has given birth to a boy! Both mother and child are safe and healthy.'

A sense of relief pervaded Fateh Mohammed and his battle-scarred face was softened by a smile. 'Have the guards announce that Fateh Mohammed has been blessed with another boy.'

'Yes, my lord.'

The son of a man of religion who had chosen a life in the military, he had risen through the ranks to be a *nayaka* – a military commander under the Nawab of Sira with fifty cavalry, 1,000 foot soldiers and a jagir – and now had a fifth son to carry on his legacy. Fateh Mohammed now had three sons from his first wife and two from Lal Bi, his second. He walked to the zenana and asked permission to enter. His female relatives stood around the bed. The newborn, wrapped in a blanket, was sleeping next to his mother.

The fair-skinned Lal Bi looked exhausted. The ordeal of childbirth hadn't taken the sheen off her beauty though. She managed a weak smile at the sight of her husband. His eyes travelled from her to their son. He was quiet, and she caught him looking at their son dreamily. 'You seem to be deep in thought, my lord. Are you wondering if he will become a holy man or a soldier?'

'I just want him to be my son, Begum.'

His first three sons had also become soldiers. His fourth son, Shahbaz, was still young. But his ancestors had been spiritual men who spent their lives in dargahs, and Lal Bi would certainly have preferred a holy man to a soldier.

'Perhaps we should consult the astrologer and find out what the stars foretell,' said Fateh Mohammed.

The bald astrologer, Ramachandra, was soon brought in to make a chart for the newborn. Even after the chart had been prepared, Ramachandra continued to peer at his creation and calculated something silently, his face expressionless. When he was finally done, he sighed before speaking. 'He is destined to be a king. A king the like of whom this land has never seen. He will forge an empire larger than any before him.' There was silence in the quarters. The astrologer looked at Fateh Mohammed and said, 'But he will soon be fatherless.'

The last prediction transformed the atmosphere of the room. Some people cursed the astrologer, while others stood mute, shocked by his prophecy. The begum, looking at her husband, burst into tears. Fateh Mohammed thanked the astrologer, paid and dismissed him.

All the women started protesting together in a cacophony of tears and grief:

'We don't need a king; you are our king, our lord and our god.'

'This baby is a harbinger of grief and pain; we don't want this child here.'

'How can we avoid the dreadful fate that this child has brought upon us?'

'Let's kill the baby and the prophecy will be averted.'

'Yes! Let's kill it!'

There was not a word of protest from Lal Bi. Her silence made it clear that she was willing to sacrifice her son for her husband.

Fateh Mohammed said with quiet determination, 'My life is in my hands. The boy has just opened his eyes to this world – he has not decided my destiny, nor should he be blamed for my fate. If God intends for me to meet him, then I will go. But I will not let anyone harm my son.'

The room fell silent. The *jagirdar* of Budikote contemplated:

What kind of prophecy was this? How could the son of a minor military commander become king? The Marathas and the nizam control everything. Anyone who dares to stand against them would be ruthlessly cut down. Is my son extraordinary in ways that I can't even fathom?

Taking his wife's hand, Fateh Mohammed said, 'Our king will need a royal name if he must tame the jackals around him. We will call him Hyder – the lion.'

For the next three years, the diplomats of Sira negotiated for peace with Nizam Asaf Jah but they eventually failed. After the monsoon of 1724, the day Fateh Mohammed had feared arrived. He had been summoned to Sira by Rasul Khan. The nizam's forces were marching from the north towards Sira on the pretext of collecting the yearly tribute from the province. At the same time, the army of Arcot was moving in from the south, and Budikote was in its path.

There was no love lost between the jagirdar of Budikote and the Nawab of Arcot. Fateh Mohammed had refused to offer his services to Saadatullah Khan. He had sworn fealty to Sira and had inflicted sizeable damage to Saadatullah Khan's forces during the skirmishes between Sira and Arcot many years ago. The Nawab of Arcot would burn the jagir down and butcher every resident linked to Fateh Mohammed, given the opportunity. Fateh Mohammed gathered his family and a few trusted retainers.

'Rasul Khan has asked me to go to Sira. We are expecting the nizam to attack. Except for Shahbaz and Hyder, my other sons will accompany me. The womenfolk will go to Doddaballapur. Kuli Khan, Rasul Khan's brother, holds that jagir. You will be safe there.'

With tears in her eyes, Hyder's mother said, 'No matter the danger or difficulty, we want to be with you. We are safer by your side than anywhere else.'

'Sira is not safe, Begum. Your safety is my priority. Shahbaz and Hyder are very young, and you must take care of them. Kuli Khan will look after you well.'

'If Sira is not safe, please don't go there. Why must you go where danger awaits? You don't owe Rasul Khan anything. Let us go to a dargah and spend the rest of our lives there.'

Fateh Mohammed's steely face softened. 'I wish I could, but I cannot do that. What we have today was made possible by Rasul Khan's father. I cannot abandon them in their hour of need. But I won't rest easy until I know you are safe. Please go to Doddaballapur and take care of our sons.'

Lal Bi knew that no amount of pleading would change her husband's mind. Resigned to this decision, the begum, muffling her sorrow, ceased arguing.

Fateh Mohammed took Hyder, all of three years old, in his arms. Kissing the child's forehead, he said, 'You take good care of your mother now.'

Hyder looked at his father with his big, bright eyes, squealed with laughter and kissed him back. All the fear in his heart vanished when he saw his father's smile and he quietly went back to his mother's arms.

The women left Budikote, taking along with them Fateh Mohammed's treasures and money, and headed towards Doddaballapur. Fateh Mohammed led his army towards Sira where Rasul Khan had asked most of his feudatories to assemble, all of whom soon arrived with their armies. Sira would be besieged shortly, and Rasul Khan was expected to lead the defence of the city.

Rasul Khan had never been a soldier. He had never led his army from the front and had no intention of leading them into battle this time either. When Fateh Mohammed arrived, he promptly handed over the responsibility of the Sira fort to his trusted nayaka and went to his ancestral dargah. But before leaving, he commanded Fateh Mohammed to protect the fort against all attacks. As Rasul Khan left Sira, the armies of Arcot and the nizam arrived on the scene.

After the monsoon of 1724, Doddaballapur

The thick *soorma*-wearing Kuli Khan of Doddaballapur warmly welcomed the group that had come knocking at his door. He was a smart man. He knew it was not in his best interests to antagonize powerful military leaders like Fateh Mohammed. He gave the women separate quarters and the respect that was due to them. Everything would have remained the same if things had turned out better at Sira.

A month passed by with no information from Sira, until late one night, when a messenger from the city arrived at the gates of Doddaballapur.

The messenger was ushered in immediately to the court of Kuli Khan, despite the hour. The court was empty, and torches were lit to brighten the otherwise dark room. Kuli Khan came in, clothed in the simple white kurta and pyjama which he had worn to bed. He had not bothered to dress up; his anxiety about the situation overrode the etiquette required for a court appearance. He enquired, 'What is the news from Sira?'

'My lord, your brother Rasul Khan had entrusted Fateh Mohammed to protect Sira. The forces of the Nizam and the

Nawab of Arcot besieged the city, but with a brave counter-attack, Fateh Mohammed's army repelled the invading forces. Unfortunately, Fateh Mohammed and his three sons were martyred during this effort.'

Kuli Khan listened to the messenger in silence. There was no grief, no expression of sorrow on his face. He dismissed the messenger and called on the courtier who had earlier lit the torches in the court.

'Summon my confidant Abbas Khan immediately.'

The courtier went out of the court, leaving Kuli Khan alone. The jagirdar sat on the teak chair that faced the door of the court. He had made up his mind and Abbas Khan was the one person he could trust to set his plan in motion.

It was a good half hour before the pudgy, olive-skinned Abbas Khan made his appearance. A man of medium height, he was dressed for court, silk covering him from top to bottom, precious stones adorning his neck and fingers. The master may not care about the etiquette of the place, but his subject was bound to maintain decorum. Kuli Khan may have called Abbas Khan his confidant, but he was essentially a slave to his master.

Abbas Khan bowed down in front of the jagirdar of Doddaballapur.

Without waiting for his confidant to speak, Kuli Khan laid out his plan.

'Fateh Mohammed and his sons have fended off the nizam at Sira. My brother has abdicated his responsibility to protect Sira, the incompetent fool! My father should have given Sira to me. Instead, I received this wretched town. At least my brother did one good thing for us – he led Fateh Mohammed and his family to their deaths.' As expected of a sycophant, Abbas Khan nodded in agreement as his master continued, 'My brother was never fit to rule Sira. The city is now lost. The nizam is bound to attack again, and I need to protect my interests. Approach the nizam and tell him that I will not lay claim to Sira as long as my claim to Doddaballapur is validated by him.'

With a wicked gleam in his black eyes, Kuli Khan continued, 'Meanwhile, I need to visit the widow of Fateh Mohammed.'

'Why, my lord?'

'Well, his treasures need a new owner now.'

A little later, the women were shocked to see Kuli Khan barge into Lal Bi's private quarters. Wasting no time with formalities, he came straight to the point. 'Begum, word has come that your husband is dead. As custom has it, you must now start paying me for my continued protection.'

The begum was stupefied; her greatest fears had come true. But Kuli Khan took no notice. He continued, 'You must pay for the hospitality that you have enjoyed until now, and that you will receive henceforth. You and your entourage will not be allowed outside your quarters until I am paid in full.'

This sudden change of circumstances was too much for the begum. She didn't know how to react to Kuli Khan's unreasonable demands. The other ladies in the quarters implored Kuli Khan to allow the begum to grieve before she could make arrangements for the payments. But he dismissed the requests and arranged his men around them in a threatening formation.

Lal Bi regained her composure and asked, 'How much must I pay you?'

'How much do you have?'

Kuli Khan knew that all the money from Budikote had travelled to Doddaballapur, but he wasn't quite sure of the exact amount. Lal Bi and her entourage were helpless and trapped in his town. In no time, he had extracted all their money and treasures. But still not satisfied, he felt that Fateh Mohammed, a favourite of his father's, must have amassed more. He was certain that Lal Bi was hiding something from him. Cajoling and verbal intimidation did not work. He had even had his men search the women's quarters every day for weeks but could not find another rupee. The coercion went on for three months, but Kuli Khan could not satisfy his greed.

Vexed, he moaned to Abbas Khan, 'She must have hidden it somewhere. Perhaps not in Doddaballapur, maybe somewhere else.' But weeks of frustration only enraged Kuli Khan further. He decided to increase the pressure on the begum.

One night, Kuli Khan and his men barged into the zenana again. The ladies were terrified of the goons who came in with the jagirdar of Doddaballapur. They huddled together, pleading for mercy. The begum, clutching her two sons, begged, 'My lord! We have given you everything we had. We have nothing else to offer. Please, be merciful!'

'Do I look like a fool? Your husband had a jagir, and I know about the riches of Budikote. You haven't parted with everything yet. Where is the rest of the money?'

The begum implored again, 'Please, my lord! We have nothing left. Look at us, look at my son Hyder. He doesn't even have a spare set of clothes. We have even given you my son's clothes. We beg you, show us some mercy!'

Kuli Khan looked menacingly at Hyder and his older brother Shahbaz. 'No more money, eh? Let's see if you will stick to this story after we take your boys.' He ordered his men, 'Grab them!'

'No! They are just children. Please spare them! Please!'

Kuli Khan's men took the two kids from the arms of the sobbing begum. The other ladies tried to stop them, but they were violently shoved aside. Three-year-old Hyder and eight-year-old Shahbaz cried and called out for their mother. As they were taken to the courtyard, the begum followed in desperation. She clutched Kuli Khan's legs, begging for her children's lives.

'Get me two *nagara*s. I want the begum to hear clearly what I want from her.'

Nagaras, percussion instruments used in times of war to raise the morale of the marching troops, were brought into the courtyard. They were to be used for an unusual purpose today. Kuli Khan ordered the skin on the instruments to be opened. 'Put the two boys inside and stitch back the skin!'

Two soldiers came forward and picked up one nagara each. They quickly removed the ropes made of cow tendons that tied the goat skin onto the wooden bowl. The goat skin was delicately removed and kept aside. The hollow bowl was large. Looking inside, the soldiers were impressed with the ingenuity of their master. The children would easily fit inside. They were looking forward to the rare spectacle. It wasn't every day that they got to torture little children.

Kuli Khan's personal bodyguards grabbed the crying boys and brought them to the middle of the courtyard where the nagaras were placed. The boys kept calling for their mother. The pleas of Lal Bi and the other women resounded in the courtyard as they clutched the legs of the soldiers who held them back. Shahbaz was hoisted and thrown into one of the wooden bowls. The bawling boy tried to climb out, but a soldier pushed him back into the bowl. The boy wouldn't give up. He tried coming out again. The soldier pinned him down while another soldier stitched the goat skin back. Then the first soldier took his hands out of the bowl as the other soldier started tying the ropes around the skin, securing it to the instrument. On seeing his elder brother being sealed inside the drum, Hyder cried out louder for his mother. Another soldier moved towards Hyder and slapped him hard. He picked up the dazed child and put him inside the other bowl. The rest of the soldiers put the skin back on. The sound of the boys' bawling was muffled now. The soldiers had done a good job of re-sealing the bowls. To the horror of the women, traditional drum beaters were brought into the courtyard while Kuli Khan's personal guards and soldiers stepped back.

Kuli Khan addressed his men, 'These ladies are not able to hear my repeated requests. They still won't tell me anything. Beat the drums! I want them to hear it clearly! Where is the money?'

The drummers picked up their sticks and started beating the drums earnestly. The entire courtyard reverberated with the beats. The begum and the other ladies were inconsolable, but there wasn't a tinge of sympathy on Kuli Khan's face. His thirst for money could not be quenched by the begum's tears. The begum could take it no longer and fainted. With the begum unconscious, Kuli Khan saw no point in continuing with the terrifying spectacle anymore. He ordered the drummers to stop and had his retainers pull the children out of the nagaras.

Shahbaz and Hyder could hardly move. Their eyes were barely open and completely red, their breathing seemed to have slowed. They were picked up and harshly thrown out of the nagaras. Kuli Khan ordered the women to take them back to their quarters and left the courtyard.

That evening, when the sun set, peace finally descended on the ladies' quarters. Hyder gripped his mother's left hand while Shahbaz clutched the right and they fell asleep in that position. They hadn't been given any food that night on Kuli Khan's orders. Sitting under the light of a candle, the begum said, 'My children will die if they stay here any longer. I need to take them away.'

The begum's companions and relatives listened to her intently as she continued, 'My husband's brother, Hydur Nayaka, is in Srirangapatna, the capital of the kingdom of Mysore. We need to seek his help. He will not let his nephews die.'

Her oldest relative, her aunt, Ayesha, said despairingly, 'But Kuli Khan will not let any of us out.'

'I am not going to let my children die here.'

'We are helpless, my child. Only the Almighty can protect us.'

'No, I will not let my children die!'

A maidservant listening to the conversation interrupted, 'I beg your pardon, my lady, but could I offer a suggestion?'

The begum nodded through her sobs.

'Kuli Khan's men are vile and immoral. They have tried to dishonour us many times. With your permission, my sisters and I will buy our way out and take your message to Srirangapatna.'

The begum was aghast. 'I cannot let my women be dishonoured by these animals. Our honour is all we have!'

'It is our duty to protect you and your kin. It will be our honour to serve you in this hour of darkness.'

While the begum was still hesitant about this plan, her relatives were more receptive. They begged her to agree as it was the children's only way out of this hell. They talked late into the night, until the begum was convinced. Over the next few days, a handful of servants got themselves out of Doddaballapur and made their way to Srirangapatna on foot.

After trudging for more than three days through drylands interspersed with scant shrubs and no food whatsoever, the ladies reached the island of Srirangapatna in the middle of a sultry afternoon. The citadel stood in front of them. They had made it.

They had no letters of credence nor jewellery to identify themselves as maids of Lal Bi. Mercifully for them, the soldiers on guard were under the pay of Hydur Nayaka, the only man who could help them. Some of the soldiers recognized the women and immediately brought them to the garrison camp near the west gate of Srirangapatna.

Hydur Nayaka was in charge of the garrison at the west gate of Srirangapatna and was living in the ramparts of the fort during the course of his roster duty. He looked like a younger Fateh Mohammed, without any scars or other ravages of war. If Fateh Mohammed had been fortunate enough to have seen better days in his life, he would have looked just like Hydur Nayaka. The pleasant smile on his face gave way to shock on seeing the servant ladies in tattered clothes, completely battered. The ladies poured their hearts out and begged him to assist their begum.

Hydur Nayaka had never thought that Kuli Khan would stoop so low. Time was clearly of the essence, and any delay would put his brother's family in further danger. With the permission of the diwan of Mysore, he marched with his personal army towards Doddaballapur. It would take his army two days to reach their destination, so he planned to start towards Doddaballapur the day he received the diwan's assent.

Meanwhile, Kuli Khan had been preoccupied with matters related to the administration of his jagir and thankfully Lal Bi and her children had been spared the torture for the next few days.

Nearly a week after he last visited Lal Bi, Kuli Khan was awakened from his sleep by Abbas Khan early in the morning.

'Hydur Nayaka's army is at the gates, my lord. I think he has come to rescue the begum.'

Kuli Khan was petrified on hearing that Fateh Mohammed's brother's army was outside his city. Just like his brother Rasul Khan, Kuli Khan was not a man of valour or honour. He realized that he would need to release the begum and her children to protect his own life. Without putting up a fight, he allowed Lal Bi and her children to join the relief army at the gates.

Hydur Nayaka was shocked to see his nephews in tattered clothes and his sister-in-law with her neck bare as they walked towards his camp. The wife of a nayaka, who should have been adorned with jewellery, looked worse than a peasant's wife. He vowed that he would never let his family be shamed like that again. He ordered his men to provide them all amenities befitting their station and set up their camp right next to his tent. The begum retold her harrowing tale to her brother-in-law. She pleaded with him to foster her children. Moved by her plight, Hydur Nayaka announced that he would take the boys under his wing and raise them as his own children.

Moving from Budikote to Doddaballapur and now to Srirangapatna had taken a toll on the two young brothers. The torture they had faced under Kuli Khan had left them in a state of shock. They seemed meek and weren't very responsive to their uncle who tried to cheer them up as they travelled.

'You are the children of Fateh Mohammed. Bravery runs in your veins. You are a soldier's sons, and you will be brave soldiers just like your father. I will personally train you to be horsemen, teach you how to use pikes and help you master the muskets. You have nothing to worry about anymore.'

Hyder was still fast asleep in his uncle's arms when they entered Srirangapatna. It was the year 1725.

2

The summer of 1749, Srirangapatna

'LOOK AT YOU! DO YOU CALL YOURSELF A SOLDIER? YOU ARE A disgrace to our family and our people.'

Twenty-seven-year-old Hyder looked at the ground as his brother Shahbaz scolded him. He had failed to come for the annual military procession – again.

'You're either hunting or chasing those dancing girls. Look at what you've become! You are a trained soldier. Your behaviour brings shame to your occupation. Come on, Hyder. You must do something with your life.'

The younger brother was still gazing at the ground. He couldn't resist the lure of big game in the forests south of Srirangapatna. But now was not the time to argue his case. He always looked up to his brother, and despite being reckless, he always tried to be in Shahbaz's good books. He had trained with his brother, and Hyder knew Shahbaz always wanted the best for him. He knew the sacrifices Shahbaz had made and was loath to disappoint him.

Shahbaz was always frustrated with Hyder but this time it was different. He was disappointed in his younger brother. Hyder sensed this change. He was not going to let his brother down.

'I am sorry, Shahbaz. I am asking for your forgiveness one last time. If you don't want to forgive me, at least punish me. I deserve it.'

'What is the point of punishing you? You won't change. You need to grow up and fulfil your responsibilities. I will not always be there for you.'

'Please don't talk like that, Shahbaz. It won't happen again, I promise. What must I do to prove that I have changed?'

But old habits die hard. No amount of cajoling and punishments would change him. The best gold comes out of the hottest fire. Only a passage through inferno would inculcate discipline, responsibility and honour in Hyder and turn him into a better man. Turning away from Hyder, Shahbaz said, 'Our diwan, Devaraja, has asked us to capture Devanahalli. I will go with Dalwai Nanjaraja to besiege the town. You will be joining me.' Without waiting for a reply, Shahbaz left the grounds, leaving his brother alone.

Hyder and Shahbaz had been taken in as military commanders under Devaraja, the Diwan of Mysore. They were allowed to have as many cavalry and foot soldiers as their father had maintained as a nayaka. Shahbaz was a chip off the old block. He was tall and well-built, just like his father. His face was regal, and like the other generals of his time, he kept a well-groomed beard and whiskers. Always draped in the finest clothes and the most delicate jewellery, he exuded an aura of authority. A true successor to Fateh Mohammed, Shahbaz raised his own army and was an important part of the Mysore force in Srirangapatna along with his uncle, Hydur Nayaka.

Hyder was not as tall as his elder brother, but he was of similar stature. Having been trained throughout his life as a man of the army, his physique was like that of any other fine soldier of the day – sturdy and strong. But unlike Shahbaz, he was clean shaven. He didn't drape himself in luxurious clothes. He didn't feel the need to project his position. He wore simple yet close-fitting white clothes and no jewellery. Despite being given the authority to raise an army, Hyder had gathered a few ragtag men and called them his army and spent all his time hunting and flirting with dancing girls. The hunting adventures had left their mark on his face: it was coarse, clearly showing that he was a man of the outdoors.

Now with Shahbaz asking to assist him during the invasion, he needed a real army if he were to make his presence felt during the attack on Devanahalli, but he didn't have one. For all practical purposes, he was just a lone volunteer under his brother in the approaching campaign.

Everywhere, preparations for the attack were accelerated. Shahbaz and his uncle were gathering their troops along with the other military commanders at the gates of the city. Supplies and bullock carts to carry them were being sourced by the civil administrators, right next to the army. Scouts were being sent out to identify suitable locations and set up temporary camps along the way to Devanahalli. Devaraja and Nanjaraja were planning the finances, diplomacy and the political consequences of the attack inside the palace.

The commander-in-chief, Dalwai Nanjaraja, was agitated. The short and thin *dalwai*, with his black hair pulled back, was pacing up and down the palace halls, while his white-haired elder brother Devaraja was calm and collected as he looked at some papers.

'That boy needled me again. The audacity of that mongrel! He thinks he can question my ability to lead the attack,' Nanjaraja thundered.

'He is your lord, Nanjaraja. He is your king – *our* king. It's his army, after all,' Devaraja tried to soothe him.

Nanjaraja looked at his brother in anger. Everyone knew that Krishnaraja Wodeyar was king in name only. All the power of Mysore resided in the hands of the brothers.

'Enough with the sarcasm, Devaraja. I need to remind that fool about the fate of his brother, Chamaraja Wodeyar.'

'Chamaraja Wodeyar took his title far too seriously. He interfered too much. I had to imprison him and send him to Kabbaladurga, the poor fellow. Couldn't take the prison air and died in a week. His brother Krishnaraja is an angel. All he does is ask you innocent questions. We can't keep sending our kings to Kabbaladurga, Nanjaraja.'

'You should have sent this *angel* to Kabbaladurga along with our previous king. Another question from him and I will personally put him in chains and let him rot to death.'

'Leave the king and the prison to me. Humour him, Nanjaraja. He needs to feel like a king from time to time. Focus on the army. This is the best time to capture Devanahalli. The Marathas are focused on the Mughals in the north, and the nizam is stuck with the Arcot affair. There is nobody to question us now.'

'The army is primed and ready. We will have the town in no time.'

'Good. Let's finish this before people start taking notice.'

The Mysore army marched through dry plains, cutting through shrubs and dry grass, as they headed towards Devanahalli. Within a few days, the walls of the town were in sight. The town may have been small, but it was well fortified. There would no doubt be a siege. Siege batteries made of logs and planks to position the cannons and provide cover for the soldiers were built at strategic points around the fort. There was no way in or out of the town now. Nanjaraja camped near the north gate with Shahbaz and some other military commanders. The south gate was covered by Hydur Nayaka and the remaining military commanders. Hyder also camped near the north gate.

Messages demanding surrender were sent to the palegar – the chief commander – holed up inside. But he refused to budge. He replied saying that he would never bow to an incompetent fool. The hot-headed Nanjaraja was offended and ordered the walls to be scaled from both sides immediately. Shahbaz was to lead from the north, and his uncle was to lead from the south.

As both sets of troops moved forward to scale the walls, the forces of the palegar attacked them from the top of the fort with their muskets. With no protection, many Mysore soldiers fell like ninepins. Amidst the skirmish, a musket ball hit Hydur Nayaka. The brave soldier fell from his horse and died at once. A sudden panic set in among the soldiers on the south side, and everyone started running helter-skelter. Messengers quickly reached Shahbaz to give him the unfortunate news.

Agitated, Shahbaz looked around, 'We need to rally the troops on the other side. Some commanders must go and stop the rout.'

If there was one thing that Hyder wanted to do in his life, it was to impress his brother. Shahbaz was more than just a sibling. He was like Hyder's father, mother, teacher, mentor and god. Until now, Hyder had offered only disappointment in return. He wanted to redeem himself in the eyes of his brother. This was his chance.

Hyder stepped forward. 'I'll go, Shahbaz. I will rally the troops.'

A few other military commanders also volunteered to go to the other side. Shahbaz selected the military commanders and said, 'You too, Hyder!'

Then he ordered a strategic retreat to the camp, as a small group of commanders raced towards the south on their horses. Hyder, on his brown horse, had a head start over the others. He whipped his horse hard and rode faster than the rest. Soon enough, he spotted the retreating soldiers.

His hunting experience was going to come in handy. He remembered his men running wildly when attacked by an elephant in *musth* or a tigress protecting her cubs. This was no different. He had to inspire the soldiers to stay put as he had done with his hunting party. Invigorated, he rushed forward.

Upon reaching the retreating soldiers, he shouted, 'Stop! Stop! Do you call yourselves soldiers of Mysore? Is this your bravery? Fall back in line! You are here to conquer and not run away like rabbits. Your general is dead. So what? I am the nephew of your general. The same blood flows through my veins. I will lead you to victory!'

Soon, the other, more experienced commanders came around, barking orders at the soldiers to fall in line. However, the soldiers looked at Hyder, who was visibly lit up with passion, for instructions. The soldiers were used to harsh but sober orders. They had never seen such fire and vigour before. They finally wound back and got behind the siege batteries. A rout was avoided, and the siege resumed.

Later that night at the war council, Nanjaraja was furiously shouting at everyone in attendance.

'How incompetent are all of you? You weren't able to capture an ordinary palegar? You disgrace my name!'

All the generals were silent. Nobody wanted to incur Nanjaraja's wrath. But the dalwai wanted a reply. Finally, Shahbaz said, 'We will have the fort for you. The troops are shaken from today's loss, but we will have them ready again. However, our cannons are not effective against the fort walls. We need to continue with the siege until they capitulate.'

'Is that our reply to that arrogant palegar? The Dalwai of Mysore bows his head to a worthless man? I will have your head cut off for suggesting such an idea!'

Hyder, who was standing behind his brother, came forward and said, 'My lord, the soldiers are baying for the palegar's blood. But I think the smarter thing to do is to use our cannons to target the zenana. I have personally seen the building when I rallied the troops near the south gate. It is very close to the gates at the south. It will be a fitting reply to his arrogance.'

'Who are you?' asked Nanjaraja.

Shahbaz replied, 'This is my brother, Hyder. He is under the employment of the diwan as a commander. He was one of the military commanders who rallied the retreating troops today. I agree with him about attacking the zenana. That will bring the palegar to his senses.'

Nanjaraja, who was still seething with anger, looked at Hyder. He saw an unshakeable confidence in the young man's face. 'Fine, then. Let Hyder take over his uncle's forces. Have the cannons target the women. I want that scoundrel's head tomorrow.' Saying this, he dismissed his party.

Hyder walked back to the camp with his brother. 'Shahbaz, you got what you wanted. The siege will continue, the dalwai got his desire. Everyone is happy.'

'You know that our cannons will barely graze the walls of the zenana, right?'

'Of course I do. But I also know of the intelligence you've received about the supplies inside the fort. They will capitulate – it's just a matter of time – and you know that.'

Impressed by Hyder's presence of mind and tact, Shahbaz teased, 'You think you are very clever? Managing our angry dalwai and foreseeing my actions?'

'I am your brother, after all. I am cut from the same cloth as you, brother. Anyway, you now need to pacify our dalwai until the fort falls.'

'Don't worry about that, Hyder. He has given you control of our uncle's troops. Keep them disciplined and stay ready.'

The siege continued for another nine days. The palegar lost hope and started secret negotiations with Shahbaz. He was willing to let go of Devanahalli in return for his family's safety. Shahbaz agreed and, in the dead of the night, the palegar escaped with his family, leaving the fort open for the Mysore army. Shahbaz ordered his brother to man the towers and the walls of the fort. By morning, Mysore had captured the fort.

A triumphant Nanjaraja walked into the fort in a grand procession. It was customary for the victorious overlord to dole out awards to his commanders, and this time would be no different. Some of the wealth from the Devanahalli treasury was distributed amongst the troops according to hierarchy. Hyder, in the lower half of the hierarchy, had to wait his turn. When his name was finally called out, he went up to Nanjaraja.

'Hyder, my boy, I am proud of what you have done. Your valour in rallying the troops after Hydur Nayaka's death should be commended. Capturing the walls and towers of the fort in one night, that was just extraordinary. You deserve more than gold and precious stones. You will take over for your uncle as one of the principal generals of the Mysore army. Moreover, I give you the authority to raise an additional 100 horses and 1,000 footmen under your command. From now on, you will be called Hyder Nayaka.'

After spending two months in Devanahalli during the monsoon, the triumphant army marched back to Srirangapatna. Devaraja was pleased with the accomplishments of his soldiers. He organized a feast for the troops the same evening. While the celebrations were underway, Nanjaraja was called to Devaraja's residence.

'Congratulations on your victory, brother.'

'A few more victories like this and we will be at the gates of Sira itself. Our borders now are closer than ever,' Nanjaraja said.

'You will need to hold your horses for now. I have received a message from the new nizam. Asaf Jah has passed away, and Nasir Jung has taken over the throne of the Deccan. However, his nephew Muzaffar Jung has also claimed the throne and has entered into an alliance with Chanda Sahib, the pretender to the seat of Arcot, to raise a rebellion against him. Nasir Jung wants us to send an army to join his standard and ravage Arcot.'

'Are we still pledging allegiance to the nizam?'

'Yes, we will pledge allegiance to everyone more powerful than us. We pledge allegiance to the nizam and the Marathas, and to the Mughals too – even if they are not aware of our existence. That's how we survive. We need to send some troops to demonstrate our fealty.'

'We just got back, Devaraja. We can't send them out again.'

'We will not send everyone. It's always a wild goose chase with the nizam. There is usually no plan, no strategy. He will simply stomp around and come back. All we need to do is send a token presence for his futile exercise.'

'We will send Hyder Nayaka and his soldiers as our representatives. That boy is good – he displayed a lot of valour at Devanahalli.'

'Hyder Nayaka?'

'You hired him, Devaraja – he is Shahbaz's brother. You must keep track of the people you hire. You never know who may turn out to be poisonous.'

'Poison doesn't kill me, Nanjaraja. Don't worry about me. Send a few junior commanders with Hyder. We will join the nizam's army at Rayakottai.'

The nizam's army was Mughal in character and size – a vast sea of men, iron and beasts shaking up the ground, ready to trample anything in its way. It had an aura of invincibility with the clattering of thousands of swords and shields. But at the same time, it was all form and no functionality. In the eyes of any military officer, it was a ragtag bunch of men with no discipline, no standard and no formation. They did not have proper uniforms or arms. Each one had his own weapon and wore his own clothes. Their movements were disorderly, raising dust everywhere. The kindest thing a military official could say was that at least some of the wealthier men dressed and moved like warriors, ready to take on the enemies on their own. The nizam's army's flanks had no cover, and their supplies were kept in vulnerable positions. They were joined by the Pathan nawabs of Kurnool, Kadapa and Savanur – Himayat Bahadur Khan, Abdul Nabi Khan and Abdul Majid Khan, respectively. These Pathans were originally from the Afghan lands. Their ancestors had migrated down south to India. They were renowned for the pedigree of their horses and their horse-riding skills. But as military troops, they were even more pedestrian than the nizam's army. The Mysore cavalry and footmen were just the same. The only island of discipline and steel were a bunch of men in red: the English had sent a contingent to support the nizam's cause.

These Englishmen had a profound effect on Hyder. He had heard a lot about them from his fellow generals, especially about their fearsome reputation of winning every battle they faced. This was his first exposure to the European military, and he immediately recognized that the Europeans had the edge when it came to the future of warfare. He was immensely impressed with their structure, movement and tenacity.

Hyder would step out of his camp every morning and evening to see the drills performed by the English soldiers. He had never seen such exercises. He marvelled at the discipline of the soldiers, their matching uniforms and the quality of their arms. As a solider by training, Hyder was keen to interact with the English and understand their ways of working, military tactics and more. But he was just a minor general of Mysore with the experience of only one battle – a small speck in the midst of generals commanding tens and thousands. The English didn't have the time to grant an audience to small-time generals like Hyder.

Even before he could push further for a meeting with them, the English left the allied forces, marching back to their capital, Madras. The English officers were unhappy with both the pace at which the nizam's army was moving towards Arcot and disgusted by Nizam Nasir Jung's lack of strategy and focus. Although, Hyder could not meet the English soldiers and commanders in person, he had decided that his personal army would be built on European lines, even though he had no idea how he would do it.

Nasir Jung supported Wallajah as the Nawab of Arcot against the claim of Chanda Sahib who, in turn, was supported by Muzaffar Jung, Nasir Jung's nephew. Chanda Sahib had obtained military aid from the French. This war turned out to be a military affair encompassing almost all the players in southern India. The vast army of the nizam and his allies trudged along the plains towards Arcot in support of Wallajah. Their movement was so slow that they had to camp and decamp for weeks. The sheer size of the army meant that marauders could attack isolated sections while they were camped without raising an alarm in the other parts of the army. So, the nizam had his allies protect the periphery of his army by having them camp on the outer edge whenever the main army camped for the night.

After weeks of marching, the nizam's army entered Arcot by nightfall. They were now in enemy territory. As the night turned darker, camp was set up and the vast army retired for the night. The allies of the nizam – Kurnool, Kadapa, Savanur, Mysore and more – camped on the outer boundaries of the main camp, a few kilometres away.

Chanda Sahib had ordered the French to attack the nizam's forces when they entered the province of Arcot. So when the nizam's army entered Arcot, the French got into action. They cut across a ridge manned by the forces of the Nawab of Kurnool in the dead of night. Surprisingly, the Kurnool forces made no effort to stop the French. After passing the Kurnool camp, the French soldiers were now in sight of the nizam's camp. They quickly took position and began an earnest attack with their muskets.

The nizam's troops panicked on seeing the French troops firing at the them. 'Raise the alarm! The French have broken through the cordon!' the soldiers shouted.

The French troops had began slashing through the sleeping army, but the nizam's troops outnumbered the French twenty to one. Soon the soldiers, awakened by the warnings that filled the air, surrounded the French. The skirmish between the two went on for hours and the French were eventually driven off, albeit with heavy losses for the nizam.

The nizam was furious with the Pathans because of their lack of action. He got on his elephant, wearing nothing but his white muslin clothes, and went towards the Kurnool nawab's tent. 'Come out, you scoundrel!' The Pathan nawab didn't emerge, so the livid nizam shouted again, 'You are true to your Pathan blood. There is not an ounce of loyalty in you. I order you, come out, right now!'

Himayat Bahadur Khan emerged from his camp, dressed in battle fatigues. He had a calm demeanour and showed no sign of fear as he faced the angry nizam. The Pathan looked straight into the nizam's eyes.

'Why didn't your troops stop the French? Answer me!' the nizam demanded.

The wizened face of the Pathan nawab displayed no emotion. He didn't break eye contact with the nizam.

'Answer me!'

Without warning, Himayat Bahadur Khan lifted the musket that was in his left hand and, gripping it with both his hands, he shot the nizam. His lifeless body fell off the elephant. The Pathan nawab calmly walked towards the dead nizam. He took a large axe from a soldier standing nearby, and in one fell swoop, he cut off the nizam's head and put it on a spike. Everyone in the camp started cheering for their master. The Pathan nawabs had struck a secret deal with Chanda Sahib, and the death of Nasir Jung was supposed to be its conclusion.

News of the nizam's murder spread like wildfire through the camp and, instead of seeking revenge, the nizam's panic-stricken army fled their camps, leaving everything behind. Almost on cue, the troops of the nawabs of Savanur, Kurnool and Kadapa looted the nizam's treasure and supplies. Even the camp followers and stragglers looted whatever had been left behind by the nizam's forces.

Hyder, posted far away from the mayhem, remained a mute spectator. Standing outside his tent, looking at the burning camp, he said, 'I don't think it's prudent for us to check on the nizam right now. I don't know who is a friend and who is a foe down there. Let's remain right here and be on our guard.'

He decided it would be best to wait for the dust to settle. After a few days, he went to the nizam's camp. Most of it was completely charred, and a few areas were still smouldering. There were rotting corpses strewn everywhere; they had attracted all sorts of critters. It was no place for people, and yet there were a few scavenging among the wreckage. Such was the size of the nizam's loot that the Pathans could not carry it all and had to leave a lot behind, which enticed the hangers-on to search for anything worthwhile.

Hyder Nayaka ordered his troops, 'Search the place. See if there is something of value.'

His forces did a quick recce and found some usable ammunition. They loaded it onto the bullock carts with their other supplies and decided to head back home. The campaign was finally over.

It had been close to a year since Hyder had seen his family. He had never had time for his family; his passion for adventure far exceeded his desire to be with them. He would rather spend time in the forests hunting than at home. But the last year had changed him. He was more determined than ever to earn his brother's respect. It had been an honour for him when his brother's benefactor, Nanjaraja, had asked him to go on a campaign with the nizam. Thus, he had readily agreed to go as Mysore's representative. But after the woeful campaign, he was disappointed about not having anything to show to Shahbaz or Nanjaraja. Riding his horse along with his troops back to Srirangapatna, Hyder felt anxious.

What will Shahbaz and Nanjaraja think of me? Will they look at me as a failure? Will Shahbaz think I am back to my old ways? But I have changed now. I just don't have anything with which I can prove to them that I have changed. I don't want to lose Shahbaz's trust. But what can I do now? The campaign is over, and I am returning empty-handed. Oh how I wish I were with my family. My mother, my wives. I want to be with them as soon as possible.

The strong urge to see his family overrode everything else in his mind. He ordered his soldiers, 'Let's cut through the forest. That should shorten our journey by a fair amount.'

Despite it being winter, it was still a hot afternoon as his army and followers moved through the forest populated by dry, leafless trees. Some of the scouts who had gone further on came rushing back with news. 'A huge line of camels and bullock carts are up further ahead. They are laden with goods and money, and they only have a nominal armed guard. We will catch up with them in an hour or two.'

'Something is not right,' Hyder thought out loud. 'But surely it can't be a trap – the bait is too big. How can they ambush anyone in this terrain? Nevertheless, we need to be on our guard. Stop our troops here. The cavalry will move ahead with me and intercept them.' Hyder and his men soon found and got ahead of the slow convoy of men and beasts, and he ordered his cavalry to attack them.

The convoy was surprised and stricken with fear when multiple horsemen started striking at them. Frozen with fear, they shouted, 'We surrender! We surrender! Please don't harm us.'

The armed escort had already dropped their weapons and were begging for mercy. The horsemen quickly rounded up the entire group and called out for its leader. A middle-aged man, more a peasant than a soldier, came to the front.

'We are only transporting the supplies of the Pathan nawabs back to their kingdoms. We are cattle herders and villagers doing the bidding of our nawabs.'

Hyder came forward and pointed his sword at him, 'What supplies?'

'I don't know, my lord. I believe it is food and clothing for the soldiers.'

'Food and clothing? Why would you travel through a forest when there is a direct road to your nawab's city?'

'Our nawab asked us to split up and move out. We were asked to come through the forest.'

'That seems like a very strange order.'

'We know nothing, my lord. We are doing as we were told.'

'Oh, then you wouldn't mind us checking your cargo.'

The man hesitated and looked helplessly at his party. Hyder's cavalry took up offensive positions. In a split second, Hyder slashed a cloth-wrapped bag in a wagon.

Precious stones – red, green, white – poured out of the bag. They glistened in the bright sun, blinding in their brilliance.

Hyder's face grew dark. Quietly, he said, 'I will give you one more chance to tell the truth.'

'Forgive me, my lord. We are camp followers of the Pathan nawabs. We thought to take some of the nizam's treasure for ourselves. We separated from them discreetly and were taking this path back to our homes. Forgive us, my lord. Spare our lives!'

The camp followers were already squatting near the legs of Hyder's horse, crying and begging for mercy. But Hyder had no mercy to spare, especially for those who lied to him. He commanded his soldiers, 'Take them back to Srirangapatna in chains.'

This was just a minuscule part of the nizam's treasures, but it was the largest haul Hyder had ever seen. One of his commanders asked him what he intended to do with it. 'The nizam is dead,' he said, so I am sure he doesn't need it.' Hyder didn't even bother to look at the loot. He ordered his soldiers to add the wagons to his convoy and resumed the journey to Srirangapatna.

When Hyder entered Srirangapatna, there were no grand celebrations like the one after the Devanahalli siege; there was only a warm welcome. The Hindu ladies of the palace removed *dhristhi* – a ritual whereby they mixed lime and turmeric with water in a plate and performed an *aarti* in front of the returning men to remove the evil eye that might have befallen the troops – before letting them inside the fort. After the religious formalities, Hyder went straight to Nanjaraja's palace.

Nanjaraja was pleased to see Hyder and greeted him warmly. 'Come in, my son. It is good to see you. I got the message of the nizam's death. He deserved it. Stupid man, he never thought with his head. I'll tell you another thing – never trust a Pathan. We must always be on our guard with them. But the Pathans are the nizam's problem. Our army is intact and that's what matters. You would have wished to taste Chanda Sahib's blood, but there is always next time.'

'Actually, this has not been a completely futile exercise. Would you care to come down to the treasury?'

Very few had ever seen Nanjaraja smile, let alone laugh. It was one of those rare days. Nanjaraja was laughing and jauntily greeting the returning soldiers. Hyder had offered the entire treasure to him. Nanjaraja was giddy with excitement. 'I am confused. Weren't we supposed to pay a tribute to the nizam? I think they have it all wrong! The Pathan nawabs will also be surprised, eh? They must be wondering why their coffers are so empty!'

Hyder merely smiled at his benefactor.

'Hyder Nayaka, I authorize you to raise 500 more horses and 5,000 men. Your men will now guard the eastern towers of Srirangapatna. Raise additional men for this purpose as well. I am proud of you, my boy! I know we will do great things together!'

After he had paid his tribute to Nanjaraja, Hyder set off to visit his family. His first wife, Asma, had become paralyzed from the hip down during childbirth. On her insistence, he had married Fatima, the daughter of the palegar of Gurramkonda. It had been four years since the wedding, but he was still childless. His mother, Lal Bi, was worried, and no sooner had he entered the zenana than she spoke her heart out. 'You don't love your mother and your wives anymore. You seem to have forgotten us.'

'Mother, I just came back from a campaign. Shouldn't you be worried about my well-being instead of complaining?'

'You are my son. Nothing in this world can harm you, my lion.' Lal Bi walked up to him and hugged him tightly. 'It is good to have you back, Hyder.'

Hyder returned her embrace. He looked towards his wives. There was relief in their eyes on seeing him safe and sound.

'Would you care to satisfy the wish of an old woman?'

'Mother, I live for you. There is nothing more important to me than your happiness.'

'When will you give me my grandchildren? I want to see your children, Hyder. You used to run away to hunt earlier, and now you only think about Nanjaraja. I'm glad that your life is more settled now, but you need an heir. I will not always be here . . .'

Asma concurred with her mother-in-law while Fatima averted her eyes shyly. Lal Bi said, 'You need to spend more time with Fatima.'

Asma added excitedly, 'There is a dargah near the city of Arcot. If the Sufi saint there blesses us, we will see little children running around the place in no time.'

Lal Bi, in full support of her daughter-in-law's suggestion, prompted, 'You should go there with Fatima, Hyder.'

'Mother, I just came back from Arcot. I am not sure if it is safe for us to go there now,' Hyder said.

But Asma was adamant. 'The dargah is renowned for helping childless marriages blossom into full families. We will go there as private citizens. Nobody is cruel enough to stop a pilgrimage to that holy place.'

Hyder could not reason with the women. He looked at Fatima, who was still looking down shyly. 'All right. We will go to Arcot and pray at the dargah.'

The family set off on the pilgrimage the same month and sought the blessings of the renowned saint at the dargah. He blessed Hyder and Fatima, assuring them that they would have a child. They vowed that if they were blessed with a child, they would name it after the saint. Within a year, in 1750, Hyder and Fatima welcomed a son into the family. As promised, they named their son Tipu in honour of the saint, Tipu Mastan Aulia.

3

The winter of 1751, Hyderabad

AFTER THE ROUT OF THE NIZAM'S ARMY AT ARCOT, MUZAFFAR Jung, the pretender to the nizam's throne, rushed back to Hyderabad. With Nasir Jung dead, there were no more obstacles in his path. He got himself anointed as the Nizam of Hyderabad with the help of his French allies. He immediately sought peace with the Pathan nawabs and promised to cede vast tracts of land to them, just as he had done with the French earlier. Enticed by the rewards they would receive, the Pathan nawabs wholeheartedly supported the new nizam. After months of celebrations, the French came to the court asking for trade concessions and lands that were promised to them. Muzaffar Jung kept his promise to the French but broke his word to the Pathan nawabs. Months of aggressive communication between the Pathans and the nizam followed, and eventually, the nizam embarked on a journey to Kadapa to meet the nawabs in person. In the midst of heated discussions, the Kurnool nawab, Himayat Bahadur Khan, speared Muzaffar Jung, killing him instantly. But Muzaffar Jung's army, unlike his uncle's panic-stricken troops, executed the Pathan nawabs. The throne of Hyderabad then passed on to Salabat Jung, the second son of the old nizam, Asaf Jah. Salabat Jung had been held prisoner first by Nasir Jung and then by Muzaffar Jung. With both of them dead and the Pathan nawabs out of the way, he was the only choice.

Within a week, Hyderabad saw Salabat Jung take the throne as the new nizam. The first decision this new nizam took was to stay away from Arcot for now and focus on strengthening himself on his home turf. And thus the kingdom of Hyderabad steered clear of regional politics for the time being.

The English, who were disgusted with Nasir Jung's poor tactics and slow pace, had retired to Madras, and focused on their primary interest, trade, albeit temporarily. Emboldened by the death of Nasir Jung and the retreat of the English, Chanda Sahib began to occupy more and more of the Arcot province, cornering his competitor Wallajah at the Trichy Fort. The French, who were actively supporting Chanda Sahib, opened siege batteries outside Trichy and mounted a constant attack on the fort.

In this moment of despair, Wallajah sent out emissaries to Mysore and the English, seeking help. The emissary sent to Mysore met Nanjaraja at his palace with a tantalizing offer, which Nanjaraja immediately presented to his brother at his palace.

'Devaraja, I presume Wallajah's emissary has met you and told you of Wallajah's proposal.'

Devaraja, in his usual calm demeanour, replied, 'Yes, and he went and met Krishnaraja Wodeyar as well. The king refused outright. I concur with our king's decision.'

'What? Are you mad? Wallajah is offering us Trichy on a platter, and you said no?'

'Listen to me, Nanjaraja. Our armies have been on the field for years now. We cannot afford another campaign. I am not sure if we can take on both Chanda Sahib and the French. Also, do you really believe that Wallajah would give up Trichy in return for our assistance?'

The rebuff from Devaraja angered Nanjaraja. Seething, he asked, 'Are you questioning my abilities and my army? Do you think I will not be able to crush that pretender and reinstate Wallajah? And what is this nonsense about agreeing with Krishnaraja? What has happened to you?'

'Patience, Nanjaraja. We shouldn't needlessly muddle already troubled waters. I don't have to agree with the king. The ambassador met the king and me separately. We both understood the improbability of his proposal. Wallajah does not control Arcot. He only has Trichy Fort. Do you think he will give it up? We can't afford another campaign either. Our treasury is running low. We should be spending more time extracting the annual tributes pending from the local palegars rather than go to Trichy.'

'I am the dalwai. I will decide if we need to go or not. And I am going to Trichy. If you won't fund the campaign, I will fund it myself using the loot from Trichy.'

Devaraja watched in silence as Nanjaraja stomped out of his palace. There was nothing that he could do. While he controlled the finances of the empire, the army answered to Nanjaraja. If the army were to march to Trichy, he could not stop them.

Back in his palace, Nanjaraja summoned Hyder Nayaka.

Hyder had completed the last rites for his mother a few days ago and was in the customary state of mourning. With both her sons having begotten heirs and settled as generals just like their father, Lal Bi had felt content with her life, having served her purpose of protecting her children. She had died peacefully in her sleep. Alone in his personal quarters, Hyder was now thinking about his mother.

She was the last of her generation. At least she left us as a satisfied woman. That's what matters in the end.

Hyder had spent a good part of the year in Srirangapatna taking care of his family. He was no longer the rash and reckless adventurer of his youth and was now a respected general and a responsible father. Still, the same fire and ambition burned in him. Asma, who had been paralyzed and in poor health, had passed away almost a year ago, a few months after Tipu's birth, and now with the death of his mother, it was just Fatima, Tipu and him. Even though he was devoted to his mother, he took her demise in his stride. He had been calm even when his uncle Hydur Nayaka had died, and this time was no different.

On hearing from Nanjaraja's courtier, Hyder immediately went to meet the dalwai.

'Son, we have another big opportunity to make ourselves rich. Wallajah has asked us to rescue him from Chanda Sahib and his mercenaries in Trichy. Once relieved, he will take over the entire province of Arcot. And he will hand over the fort to us,' Nanjraja said.

Hyder found it hard to believe that Wallajah would keep his promise.

Why would Wallajah hand over Trichy to us? That doesn't make sense.

He didn't question Nanjaraja's decision, however, and Nanjaraja went on, 'Get your forces ready. We will march on Trichy at the earliest.'

'Yes, my lord.'

And soon, Nanjaraja, despite the king's direct denial of permission, readied the entire Mysore army for the campaign, leaving only a small force behind to protect Srirangapatna.

In Trichy – a city in Arcot on the banks of the Kaveri River – most of the activity revolved around the temple on the river island of Srirangam. Wallajah himself was holed up in a fort south of the island, on the southern bank of the river. Chanda Sahib and his forces had taken control of the island and set up strong siege batteries south of the fort. When the Mysore forces arrived, there was no strong ground for them to challenge the besiegers. So, they took the only option available to them. They camped on the northern bank of the river.

Mysore's army was separated from whatever little troops Wallajah held in the fort by the river, making a joint attack against Chanda Sahib nearly impossible. Nanjaraja's generals advised him against a direct attack on Chanda Sahib as he held the stronger ground with an equally strong army.

Meanwhile, Wallajah had also sought the assistance of the English. Since Trichy had already been besieged by Chanda Sahib and the French, the English thought the best course of action was to create a diversionary tactic. They sent a minor clerk named Robert Clive with a small force to attack Chanda Sahib's capital, Arcot. Surprisingly, Clive was able to take over the city despite being outnumbered ten to one. Alarmed by the loss of his capital, Chanda Sahib dispatched a large force under his son to take back the city. The balance was now tilted in favour of the Mysore army in Trichy.

Nanjaraja called his war council to plan their course of action. 'Some of Chanda Sahib's army has been called away. This is a good time to attack the remaining troops and capture the fort.'

Shahbaz, who was in the council, said, 'It won't be easy to dislodge the French. They are much tougher opponents than Chanda Sahib's troops. Also, they are constantly attacking the walls of the fort, striking fear and lowering the morale of all those inside the fort. We need to stop their gunfire before taking any further steps.'

'All right, we will first address the French cannons. Hyder, get your troops together and find a way to take out those cannons.'

Hyder, already impressed with the European forces, was not very confident about winning against the French. The cannons were protected by the French infantry. If he did attack them, Chanda Sahib might come to their assistance. He needed to come up with an effective strategy to overcome the French.

I have more men and horses. But my numerical superiority does not give me an advantage. My light armoured cavalry, the kuzzaks, are more skilled at guerrilla warfare than pitched battles. So, in the present scenario, they will definitely be killed by the determined French infantry. But since my kuzzaks are lightly armoured, they will be fast. Their advantage over the French is speed. I need to make the best use of it. A fight in daylight would mean the French could manoeuvre their infantry to overcome the speed of my cavalry. A night attack by my kuzzaks would be best. That's the solution!

Every day, the French cannons bombarded the walls of Trichy Fort. At nightfall, the cannons would stop firing, and the French soldiers would go back to their camps. A few days after being given the order by Nanjaraja, Hyder collected the best of his horses, crossed the Kaveri in the dead of the night and moved behind the French cannons. Under the cover of darkness, he unleashed the kuzzaks at the unsuspecting French soldiers.

Hyder's cavalry moved swiftly towards the French camp. By the time the night guards saw the approaching horses and raised an alarm, it was too late. The horses crossed over the barricades, and the men set a few tents on fire. But the French soldiers were quick on their feet, and despite the losses, they were able to regroup to challenge the cavalry. Hyder ordered a tactical retreat of the kuzzaks. The French soldiers gave them chase, but the horses were just out of the reach of their muskets.

With most of the French soldiers out of the camp, the second phase of Hyder's attack had begun. A smaller cavalry unit rode into the camp, went over to the siege battery and stole away four cannons. Using makeshift bamboo boats, they were transported back to the Mysore camp. The retreating kuzzaks were informed of the successful completion of the second phase and they too returned to the camp. The French siege machinery may have been unstoppable, but they had been slowed down for now.

The Mysore camp erupted with joy on seeing the captured cannons. Nanjaraja, once again impressed with his protégé, awarded him even more horses and footmen. But Hyder's mind was still on the cannons.

These cannons are far more precise than any of the cannons in the Mysore army. They are better built and don't crack open from the intense heat produced by a few blasts of cannon balls.

His fascination for the Europeans turned to admiration.

I have always known that the French troop structure, movement and discipline have been superior to ours. But even their military equipment is in a league of its own. They are next to invincible on the battlefield.

Hyder's resolve grew even stronger: only an army built on European lines could rule over these lands.

A few days later, in the Arcot camp, Chanda Sahib received news that his relief army sent to recapture Arcot had been defeated by Robert Clive, and his son had been killed in action. The siege at Trichy was going nowhere, he'd lost his capital city and his son, and now he didn't even have a large enough army to take on the challenge from Mysore. Fearing for his life, he rushed to Thanjavur for safety. But fate had something else in store for him.

Many years ago, Chanda Sahib had occupied the temple city of Madurai. The city's nayaka, Trimuk Nayaka, had already pledged allegiance to him and was out on a mission to Thanjavur. Chanda Sahib falsely promised the nayaka that his family would be safe. In the absence of the nayaka, he violated his wife Munka Rani and then brutally killed her. Trimuk was helpless against a powerful overlord like Chanda Sahib and was forced to resign to his fate. Now, Chanda Sahib's distressed arrival in Thanjavur offered him a rare and much-awaited opportunity to avenge the death of his wife. Soon enough, assassins from Madurai secretly arrived in Thanjavur and Chanda Sahib paid his debt to Trimuk Nayaka with his life. With the death of the Nawab of Arcot, there was no competition to Wallajah's claim to the Arcot throne.

After hearing about Chanda Sahib's death, the French saw no reason to continue with the siege and promptly returned to Pondicherry. With the siege over, Wallajah was declared the Nawab of Arcot and the Mysore army was at the gates of Trichy, waiting for their reward.

Nanjaraja sent a letter to Wallajah asking him to honour his word of handing over the fort to Mysore. The new nawab tried to stall the handover, but the impatient Nanjaraja would not wait and sent another strongly worded letter asking for the keys to the fort. Wallajah caved and promised to hand over the keys to Nanjaraja's most trusted aides the following morning.

Later that day, Wallajah's reply was discussed in Nanjaraja's war council. 'We need to send some generals to the fort to complete the handover.'

A general asked, 'How many soldiers can we take? We need them to man the towers and the gates after the handover.'

Nanjaraja explained that Wallajah had specifically said that he would not allow any soldiers to enter the fort – except for personal retainers.

There was disquiet in the group, but Nanjaraja remained confident. He said, 'There is nothing to worry about; our army is right outside the gates. Wallajah won't try anything. He has asked me to send the aides tomorrow morning. Hyder Nayaka will lead the group.'

Shahbaz, who had been silent all along, rose to speak. 'I think Hyder should remain with you. He is a little hot-headed, and we need someone level-headed to finish the task. I would like to volunteer.'

Nanjaraja stared at Shahbaz and wondered:

Is he jealous of Hyder Nayaka? Does he want all the glory of the capture of Trichy? Shahbaz has been a loyal servant. Perhaps I have been focusing too much on Hyder and ignoring Shahbaz. I should entertain his request and keep him in good humour.

'All right, Shahbaz, you will lead our delegation. Hyder will remain with me.'

Later that night, Hyder went to Shahbaz's tent. 'Why did you do that, Shahbaz? Is everything all right?'

'I don't trust Wallajah's intentions. I think this is a trap.'

'Then why are you going? I will go to the fort, Shahbaz. I will be on my guard. Our army is outside in any case. Wallajah will be digging his own grave if he tries to harm us.'

'It's better if I do the talking. You are in a better position to protect me if you are outside than the other way around.'

Hyder couldn't persuade his brother to change his mind, so he retired to his tent, reluctantly accepting his Shahbaz's decision.

The following morning, the Mysore delegation, comprising a few generals, including Shahbaz, and their personal retainers, entered the fort. Wallajah, who had warmly welcomed them into his residence earlier, promptly imprisoned them and shut the gates of the fort.

Now that he had the top generals of Mysore under his control as a bargaining chip, he was confident that the fort would remain in his hands. He sent a message conveying his true intentions to Nanjaraja. The Dalwai of Mysore was livid. Not only did he not get the fort, he had also lost some of his key aides.

A furious Nanjaraja addressed the rest of his generals, 'That scoundrel! Is there no honour in this world anymore? He will pay for this! Occupy the grounds where the French were stationed. Direct all our cannons, including the ones we stole from the French, at the Trichy walls. Show them no mercy!'

The relieving force had now become the besieging force. But the Mysore army didn't have proper siege batteries, nor was it large enough to enforce a siege. It became more of a blockade than an airtight siege. Though Trichy couldn't move freely out of the fort without facing the Mysore army, Wallajah managed to send messages to the English seeking their help. The English were still on his side but could not spare troops to rescue their trapped allies. Instead, they offered to transport supplies from Thanjavur to Trichy. With his army watching the fort like a hawk, Nanjaraja managed to receive intelligence about this plan.

'We need to stop those supplies from reaching Wallajah or our siege will mean nothing. That mongrel will feed on Thanjavur rice while we eat grass in this godforsaken place. Never! I want him to suffer!'

Confident about the capabilities of his kuzzaks, Hyder volunteered to intercept the supplies. He took his entire light cavalry and the fastest foot soldiers south towards the rice bowl of the region, Thanjavur.

The English convoy from Thanjavur to Trichy was long and heavily guarded. They were already on the move with money, ration, ammunition and other materials. Hyder knew that he would not be able to stop the convoy in one go. The heavily armed English soldiers would be able to take out his kuzzaks in a direct fight in no time. And the risk of getting too close to Thanjavur, which was also hostile to Mysore, was not lost on him. Fortunately for Hyder, the supply caravan was following a long, predefined path, which would make it easy for the kuzzaks to carry out raids without a counter-attack from the English. So, Hyder ordered the kuzzaks to attack the convoy wherever the security was thinner and the exit options were quick. The kuzzaks soon swung into action.

Early in the afternoon when the sun was high up in the sky, the English convoy, having finished their lunch, were slowly moving towards Trichy. The heat was intense, and it slowed down the bullocks further. Looking ahead at the horizon, the English soldiers noticed dust rising. 'This must be a hostile force,' said the commander.

The troops quickly got into formation. As they did so, the civilians in the convoy pointed out that dust was rising in two other directions as well.

'We are surrounded!'

In no time, the ground started shaking. The civilian suppliers were no soldiers and they cowered in fear.

Despite orders to get into a square formation, the suppliers were too afraid to move. The kuzzaks had arrived, and they clearly outnumbered the English soldiers. They encircled the disbanding convoy, brushing away the smattering of musket shots that the English soldiers fired. In no time, the soldiers defending the convoy were either killed or forced to retreat. The suppliers were more than ready to run back to Thanjavur, leaving everything behind. With the suppliers and the rest of the convoy on the run, the footmen of the Mysore army quickly entered the scene and gathered all the abandoned supplies. Then they rushed back to the makeshift Mysore camp before the next part of the convoy, with its English sepoys, reached the same location.

The raids were carried out at different times of the day. There was no pattern, no warning. Sometimes the attack took place early in the morning and at other times it took place at night when the convoy was asleep. But they happened on an almost continuous basis. Within a few days, Hyder was able to amass enormous amounts of gold, silver, ammunition and other loot.

The English were not able to track down the Mysore cavalry because they were much faster and kept changing their bases. They could neither stop the convoy to regroup as it was important to reach Trichy at the earliest. Nor could they move any faster as they were carrying a lot of supplies. The only thing they could do was to keep the convoy moving and deliver whatever remained of the goods taken during the raids.

For more than six months, these raids led by Hyder helped him amass a vast fortune. But he was an illiterate man who knew more about military tactics than about accounts and finances. He now needed someone to manage this wealth. Late one evening, after yet another successful raid, when he was in his tent with his generals and other officers, he said, 'I don't know how much we have looted or what that loot is. I only see mounds of bags in our camp. I will not even know if someone steals from us.'

A short, pudgy man, who was clearly bald but had covered his head with a yellow turban, came forward and said, 'I have maintained accounts of the loot, my lord.' The man held out a bunch of papers towards Hyder and continued, 'This is an itemized list of the gold, silver and precious stones that you acquired in the last few days.'

Hyder looked at him with narrowed eyes.

Sensing the nayaka's suspicion, the man realized that he hadn't introduced himself.

'My name is Khande Rao, my lord. I have been part of your office since your Arcot campaign. I am an accountant by learning who is working as a clerk under you, my lord. I took the liberty to create accounts for the last few days to ensure that there was no loss to you. With your permission, I can show you the accounts that I have prepared.'

It was standard practice for generals to take even the administrative members of their offices along with them on campaigns. Khande Rao was one among many such clerks who were part of this campaign. Hyder was not one to care about hierarchy, class or titles. He was only interested in what Khande Rao had to say and made the man read out his record of the raids line by line.

With the complete account spelled out, Hyder closed his eyes and thought for some time. When he opened his eyes, he said, 'Well done, Khande Rao, I am impressed. You will be my accountant from here on. I want an inventory of everything, including clothes, rations and ammunition we have in our possession now. Make records of what needs to be provided to the troops as well.'

After that, the raids continued. In this battle of attrition, no one blinked or conceded defeat. Days turned into weeks, weeks into months. Hyder continued with his aggrandizement while the English pushed supplies with no regard for the money or men they lost. Back in Trichy, Wallajah was surviving on whatever meagre supplies had managed to reach him.

Wallajah had closed the gates of the fort to Nanjaraja out of his own volition, but the dalwai kept the nawab inside for three years against his will in retaliation. Now the blockade had started taking a toll on Nanjaraja too. The harsh conditions outside Trichy affected his health adversely. He was also disturbed by the betrayal and the capture of his best general, Shahbaz. The fact that he had defied everyone to undertake this doomed campaign was still heavy on his mind. Nanjaraja was not ready to give in, but his body was not in agreement with his mind. His health was deteriorating with every passing day. And things were about to get worse.

The winter of 1754, Trichy

One foggy morning, nearly four years after the Mysore army first entered Trichy, a lone horseman raced towards the Mysore camp outside Trichy Fort. The siege had sapped the energy of most soldiers and the thick fog had prevented them from realizing that someone had entered the camp. The horseman rode straight to the biggest tent, where he was stopped by the guards outside. Upon proving and declaring his identity, he was immediately let inside. The man was a messenger from Srirangapatna with an urgent message for Nanjaraja.

Later that morning, when the sun had risen and the fog had lifted somewhat, Hyder visited a grim Nanjaraja in his tent. 'Sit down, son,' said Nanjaraja. 'Things are not well at home, and I need to get back to Srirangapatna. Devaraja has sent a message that the nizam had laid siege to our capital and is demanding the annual tribute. I need to be there at the earliest. You take over the blockade. I will go home with my personal army. You can take over Shahbaz's troops as well.'

The news was sudden. A concerned Hyder suggested that all of them must return to Srirangapatna and reclaim it from the nizam.

'The city is safe for now, son. Devaraja has emptied the coffers and paid the nizam. There was nobody to protect the city.'

He paused for a moment. In a trembling voice, Nanjaraja said, 'I should have been there. I am the Dalwai of Mysore, and I was not there in its time of need. Everybody now knows that Srirangapatna is poorly defended. I need to get back before another calamity befalls our capital.'

'We all need to go back – we need to be at our full strength. One never knows when there will be another attack,' Hyder insisted.

'Srirangapatna is my responsibility, son. You continue with the siege.'

'We have been stuck here for months now. I don't think we will be able to break Wallajah. Let's go home.'

'What? Break the siege? I didn't spend so much time and money to give up now. How could you say something like that, Hyder? I thought you were different. I thought you were brave.'

'My brother Shahbaz is being held prisoner inside the fort. He is my life, and I am willing to move heaven and earth to bring him back safely. But I know that the siege will not help me get him back. I know the value you see in Trichy. I know you want to punish Wallajah. My lord, your wish has always been my command, but this siege is not going to help you achieve anything. We will get Trichy, I promise you. But it will be on another day, not today.'

Nanjaraja saw reason in Hyder's words and calmed down. He said, 'I will go back to the capital, and you raise the siege and go to Dindigul. It is the outermost district of Mysore and has been without a commandant for some time now. Take over Dindigul and raise revenues to run the district. I would like to salvage at least something worthwhile from this woeful campaign.'

Nanjaraja wound up his camp and began marching towards Srirangapatna. After a few days, Hyder started towards Dindigul down south, vowing to himself that he would bring his brother back. With the addition of his brother's troops, he was now the most powerful general in Mysore; his army was strong enough to stand on its own. This was the army that marched into Dindigul, a district abutting the enemy territory.

Despite the upheaval caused by Nanjaraja's Trichy campaign, Dindigul had remained loyal to Mysore. Hyder was warmly welcomed into the fort. This was the first time he was taking charge of a district independently. He had never even commanded a fort before, let alone a district. The challenge now was not military but administrative. He had to move into the role of a civil administrator from that of a military general.

He immediately went about understanding the administrative, security, revenue and other procedures from the local officials. Within three months, he had gained a good grasp over all things administration, and soon he got Dindigul's administrative apparatus working like a well-oiled machine.

Five months after his arrival in Dindigul, Hyder was in the middle of a revenue discussion with the treasury officers when Khande Rao, who was part of the meeting, spoke. 'My lord, I have been going through the accounts. You have a large army, and paying them requires income. You will not receive huge amounts of money frequently like we did from our raids on the English. I recommend that you channel funds from Dindigul's revenue to sustain the army.'

'The revenue belongs to Mysore, Khande Rao.'

'And you are the servant of Mysore, my lord. Your strength is the strength of the kingdom. Now is the time to strengthen yourself in order to strengthen Mysore.'

Hyder gave the idea some thought and acquiesced to Khande Rao's suggestion.

But Khande Rao was not finished.

'There is one more thing that needs your attention, my lord. The palegars who have pledged allegiance to Dindigul haven't paid their tributes for a few years now. It would be prudent to employ your army to extract these tributes. The money obtained would prove useful when strengthening your position in the Mysore Empire.'

Before Hyder could respond, Khande Rao added, 'This is to strengthen Mysore of course, my lord.'

Over the next few months, Hyder systematically extracted tributes from all the palegars. Some were cajoled, some coerced and others intimidated. Once the revenues of Dindigul were streamlined, its coffers were filled in no time. Next, Hyder secretly negotiated the release of his brother for a hefty ransom.

However, Shahbaz seemed to have had an epiphany during his captivity. He wrote a letter to his brother saying that his military days were over, and he was going to take his family to Kolar and become a holy man in a dargah, like their ancestors. And this is how, Shahbaz gave his army to Hyder, who was taken aback by his brother's decision. Nonetheless, he respected Shahbaz's wishes. Since there were many things happening in Dindigul which needed his immediate attention, Hyder chose not to travel and meet his brother in Kolar. He thought he would meet him on his way back to Srirangapatna.

Officials from Dindigul also put him in touch with French artificers who were active in the region. Hyder had been wanting to interact with the Europeans for a few years now, and he finally had the opportunity to do so. He lost no time in hiring them to modernize the defences of the Dindigul fort. He then used these men to open a channel of communication with the French administration. All he had to do now was to wait for a signal from the dalwai to start the negotiations to modernize the entire Mysore army. He had been waiting for this all along – an army modelled on European lines.

Things had never looked better for Hyder. It was then that he received a message from Nanjaraja requesting his presence in Srirangapatna.

4

The winter of 1755, Srirangapatna

NANJARAJA HAD ARRIVED AT THE GATES OF SRIRANGAPATNA a month after leaving Trichy. There were no remnants of the siege around the fort. When the troops entered the gates, they were greeted by a sombre environment, but there were no signs of bloodshed or death. The dalwai ordered his troops to break formation and dismissed them.

Nanjaraja entered the palace to find his elder brother sitting all alone in the court hall. His unkempt beard and frayed white hair made Devaraja look much older than he actually was.

'My apologies, Devaraja. I was not here during the kingdom's hour of need. There is no excuse for my absence.'

'The hour of peril has passed, Nanjaraja. We are safe now, but the fear of being without security still lingers.'

'I am here now, Devaraja, and so is the army. Srirangapatna is safe.'

'Nanjaraja, both of us know that we cannot stand up to the nizam. Our army is just a drop compared to the ocean that is the nizam's army. The only way to survive is by pledging our allegiance and paying tributes. We paid a tribute this time as well. Even after emptying our treasury, we were not able to meet the nizam's demands. Krishnaraja Wodeyar personally intervened, gave away his personal jewels and bought peace with the nizam. Our king is extremely displeased with you. Despite his objections, you went ahead to Trichy. You did not collect the tributes from our vassals. Our treasuries were not replenished. It was an extremely humiliating experience for Krishnaraja Wodeyar to pledge his jewels to the nizam. He questioned your capabilities and decisions. You rushed to Trichy thoughtlessly. And what did you bring back from there? Nothing.'

Nanjaraja's eyes turned red. He clenched his teeth to prevent himself from exploding in anger. He was silent for a few seconds, but he could take it no longer and burst out, 'That's it! Krishnaraja Wodeyar has overstepped his limits. I won't take orders from a puppet.'

Devaraja rose in anger, 'Enough! The king is right! Despite our pleas, you went on a fool's errand to Trichy. You ran our reputation into the ground, and you have put the very existence of Mysore in danger. Your army can't protect us, Nanjaraja.'

Nanjaraja was stunned by his brother's reply. His anger and fury vanished in an instant. He turned cold. His silence was unsettling, like the calm before a storm. He asked softly, 'Tell me, are you on my side or the king's side?'

'You are insane! You don't listen to anybody. Only a fool would side with you.'

Nanjaraja's demeanour was still calm. 'I have had it with Krishnaraja Wodeyar. I will not hesitate to kill anybody who crosses my path – whether he be a king or my brother.'

Devaraja froze where he stood. Nanjaraja didn't even wait for his response and stormed out of the palace. Realizing his life was in danger, Devaraja informed his retainers and sent word to the king that he would be heading to his jagir outside the capital, ostensibly to unwind after the nizam affair. The very next day, Devaraja was out of Srirangapatna. He did not want to be killed. Nor did he want to be associated with any plot or rumour of regicide.

But the disagreement between the brothers had already become the talk of the town. They were convinced that Nanjaraja would kill Krishnaraja – it was only a question of when. The rumours grew louder, making Nanjaraja realize that it would not be prudent to kill the king at the moment. He needed Devaraja by his side before taking any drastic action.

Within a few weeks, after Devaraja left the capital, Nanjaraja sent messengers to his brother, requesting him to return to the capital. Even though Krishnaraja Wodeyar was alive and healthy and the rumours had started to die down, Devaraja feared for his own life. He felt he could no longer trust his own brother. He was sure that he would be assassinated by Nanjaraja if he went back to Srirangapatna. At times he feigned sickness and at other times he said that he was being held up by pressing matters in his jagir, every time a messenger arrived from the capital. But Nanjaraja persisted with his messages. He kept telling his elder brother about the need for a competent diwan to steer the empire. He also expressed regret for his harsh words and promised that he would not harm Krishnaraja Wodeyar. Gradually the stream of messages softened Devaraja's stance. Nanjaraja's perseverance seemed to pay off. Sensing a change of heart in his brother, Devaraja returned to Srirangapatna. And just when everything seemed to have returned to normal, Devaraja died of poisoning, two days after his return. Nobody could confirm who had poisoned him or why but everyone had their suspicions.

Nanjaraja was now the Dalwai and the Diwan of Mysore. In other words, he had become the de facto ruler of Mysore.

Devaraja was cremated with full state honours with Nanjaraja personally leading the way. The kingdom would have gone into official mourning had they not received intelligence that the Marathas were planning to attack them. Mysore had not paid the chauth for some time, and the Marathas, along with their fearsome army, were coming to collect their dues.

It was a rude introduction to kingship for Nanjaraja. His first task as the diwan was to fend off arguably the most powerful military in India with an army that was not at full strength and no match for the war machinery of the Marathas. The treasury was empty, and there was no way to pay the dues even if he wanted to. Unlike the nizam, the Marathas were more than willing to use force to achieve their goals. They would rather burn Srirangapatna to the ground than waste time on protracted negotiations. Nanjaraja knew this. His own life would be in grave danger if he angered the Marathas. He immediately sent a message to Hyder, asking him to return to the capital while he pondered how to pacify the Marathas.

The Maratha army was probably the only one that matched – if not surpassed – the nizam's army in terms of sheer numbers. Unlike Salabat Jung's army, which had more infantry, the Marathas invested in the cavalry. The cavalry numbered in the thousands, ranging from irregular mercenaries, or *pindaris*, to the heavily armoured guards of the generals. Almost all their generals were cavalrymen. The arrival of the Marathas in one's territory was like seeing hell's gates open. The pindaris, who formed the forward guard, would start with indiscriminate looting and senseless murder. Next, the main cavalry would trample anything and everything that managed to stand up to them after the plunder of the pindaris.

The moment Nanjaraja received news that the pindaris had entered Mysore territory, he quickly sent his ambassadors to the Maratha camp right outside the border. The Marathas knew that Mysore was in a weakened position and were able to extract the maximum penalty from Nanjaraja. Almost all the territories Mysore had captured in the old Sira province were pledged to the Marathas. The revenue from these districts was to be used to pay the chauth. To ensure this happened, all the forts in this region were to be garrisoned by Maratha soldiers.

This was another humiliating blow to Nanjaraja. He had displayed a lack of military prowess by failing to capture Trichy; he had failed in his duty as dalwai by not being there during the nizam's threat; and now, as the Diwan of Mysore, he was unable to protect its districts. He suddenly missed the counsel of his elder brother. He felt alone in his palace, alone in Mysore, all alone in his life. 'Devaraja would have never allowed this to come to a head. His wise counsel would have helped me tide over this situation.'

But the worst was yet to come.

He had not paid the troops that had accompanied him for his Trichy campaign. Everyone knew there was no money in the treasury and now, with parts of Mysore being pledged away, not much money would be forthcoming to the treasury. The soldiers turned mutinous and started demanding their pay. Nanjaraja was now confined to his palace, surrounded by soldiers who grew more and more aggressive as the days passed.

The only person Nanjaraja trusted now was his protégé, Hyder Nayaka. He spent his days frantically waiting for Hyder to come to his aid. It was in these times of turmoil that Hyder and his forces marched into Srirangapatna. Despite the menacing mood of the agitated troops, Hyder was allowed to meet Nanjaraja. No one wanted to go up against his large army.

On entering the palace, Hyder was shocked to see the state of his mentor. Nanjaraja was a shell of his former self. His anger, passion and energy were all but gone. He looked like a crumpled blanket, sitting on his masand. Hyder entered Nanjaraja's quarters and bowed, greeting his mentor.

Seeing Hyder sent a shot of energy surging through Nanjaraja's veins. He quickly rose and hugged Hyder.

'My boy, I am so glad to see you! You must have heard all about the troubles that plague me. I am being held prisoner in my own home, son.'

'I heard about the pay dispute, and I can see the treatment they have meted out to you. Don't worry, I will personally settle the dues and handle this situation.'

A huge burden was lifted off Nanjaraja's chest. 'I knew I could count on you. You have done more than my kin have done for me – you are my only family now.'

'Leave your soldiers to me. Please take care of yourself – you look so weak and tired. I will come back with good news.'

Hyder asked all the mutinying soldiers to assemble in the city centre. He got on a makeshift stand and addressed them. 'I know your pain, and I have come to ease your suffering. You will receive your hard-earned money right now. You will never be disappointed as long as I am around. That's my word to you.'

The gathered soldiers cheered loudly. Hyder continued, 'I will have my accountants brought here. Tell them what your dues are, and after scrutinizing your accounts, we will make the payments right away.'

This announcement was met with unbridled joy. Hyder's soldiers had to jostle with the cheering troops to keep them in order. Hyder Nayaka took Khande Rao aside and said, 'Scrutinize each demand and make the payments from my personal treasury. Pay extra if necessary but disband the more troublesome ones. I don't want these shenanigans to happen again.'

By evening, the whole city was reverberating with only one name.

'Long Live Hyder Nayaka!'

'Dalwai! Dalwai! Hyder for dalwai!'

The sounds of the cheers reached Nanjaraja. Hyder had done the impossible. He had managed to pacify the mutinous troops and turned them into a bunch of fawning devotees.

Later that night, a victorious and drunk Hyder staggered into Nanjaraja's palace. Clearly, he too had been celebrating with the soldiers.

'I did not send for you, Hyder. It's late, and I see that you also are enjoying your success. I am not sure if we can have a meaningful conversation,' Nanjaraja said.

Hyder spoke incoherently. The alcohol had taken over his mind and tongue. With great difficulty, he bowed before his mentor. 'You summoned me, my lord.'

Nanjaraja saw the son he always desired in Hyder, so he readily forgave this transgression.

He can celebrate his success. He deserves it. I would have celebrated the same way if I had managed to do what he has done today. I am proud of what my son has achieved today.

Smiling at his protégé, Nanjaraja said, 'I have heard the calls for making you the dalwai. I am more than happy to appoint you the commander of the Mysore army – I am not as greedy as people think. I will announce your elevation tomorrow. Go ahead and enjoy the rest of the night.'

A few weeks later, the new Dalwai of Mysore, Hyder Nayaka, requested a meeting with Nanjaraja. 'I was told by the revenue department officials that we have pledged all our districts near Sira to the Marathas in lieu of the chauth. That was not a prudent decision, my lord' he said.

'What was I supposed to do, Hyder? The very existence of Mysore was at stake. I had to yield to their demands!' Nanjaraja protested.

'If I may, I could offer a solution here. The Marathas do not have a presence in Sira anymore. Except for a small garrison here and there in our forts, they are not to be found anywhere. We must recapture our districts. Our treasury is running low, and we need to extract as much revenue as possible. We can't let our own districts lie idle.'

'The Marathas will soon be back, baying for our blood.'

'We don't have the money to pay chauth year after year. We will end up pledging more districts and soon there will be no Mysore left to speak of. I suggest we take back the districts and fill our treasury at the earliest. We will worry about the Marathas when they are at our gates.'

Nanjaraja sighed, 'You are the dalwai. It is your decision.'

With Nanjaraja's permission, Hyder sent his army to flush out the Marathas from the occupied districts and deployed Khande Rao to extract tributes and revenues from all these places. Khande Rao turned out to be extremely effective, albeit cruel, while extracting revenues. While he encouraged the use of overwhelming forces against every palegar who had sided with the Marathas and emptied their treasuries, he showed no empathy for the concerns and difficulties of the jagirdars who had not supported the Marathas and had to face the brunt of their formidable army either. Money was the primary objective for Khande Rao. Soon, the treasury of Mysore was filled to the brim and all the districts and major forts were under Hyder's control. He left men loyal to him at all these places. For all practical purposes, Hyder Nayaka now controlled Mysore. He had truly taken over from Nanjaraja.

Maratha soldiers flushed out by Hyder soon reached Poona and informed Peshwa Madhav Rao about Mysore's actions. Rebellion against the Marathas was unacceptable. At his palace in Poona, Peshwa Madhav Rao pondered:

If this kind of transgression is allowed, every man, fort and city would raise a banner of revolt against the power of the Marathas. I need to instil fear in the heart of Mysore lest they think that they can get away with such rebellions.

The peshwa personally took charge of his army and marched down to Mysore.

The main Maratha army camped just inside the border of Mysore. The pindaris were sent to ravage the land. But things were different this time. They were put to the sword by Hyder's kuzzaks. Sensing a change in the character of his adversary, Madhav Rao sent his main cavalry and infantry to scare the enemy light cavalry away. As expected, the kuzzaks offered no resistance. The invading Maratha army quickly blockaded Bangalore and Channapatna, the two cities close to Srirangapatna. They wanted to slowly choke the capital by cutting off supplies and people from these cities before they began the siege in eanest.

But Hyder was one step ahead of the Marathas. He had placed his loyalists in the two cities. They chose to withstand the blockade rather than yield. Back in Srirangapatna, Hyder assembled his war council.

'The Marathas are at Channapatna and Bangalore. Lutf Ali will lead the charge at Channapatna. Harass them, give them hell. Make them regret entering Mysore. I will lead the charge in Bangalore. We will use the French cannons we procured at Dindigul. May God be with us!'

The short-statured Lutf Ali Beg, a general with salt-and-pepper hair and a clean-shaven face, bowed to Hyder, accepting the task assigned to him.

The next morning, Lutf Ali, dressed in full military armour, led his army out of Srirangapatna to face the Marathas at Channapatna.

Within a span of three days, Hyder assembled his foot soldiers, kuzzaks and the French cannons, and began marching towards Bangalore. Two days after leaving Srirangapatna, he was at the Bangalore fort. The Marathas had camped north of the fort and Hyder camped on the opposite end. The siege equipment of the Marathas was inferior and had barely made a dent on the walls of the fort. Hyder started firing their much more superior cannons at the Maratha troops while his kuzzaks harassed the foraging parties that came out of the Maratha camp. The Marathas were facing a two-front battle with Hyder on the outside and the besieged forces inside.

Despite Hyder's relentless attacks, the Marathas were still overwhelmingly superior in numbers and arms. The siege of Bangalore was going nowhere; it became a hit-and-run game where the kuzzaks would attack the foraging parties and the Maratha cavalry would chase away the much faster kuzzaks. In the meantime, news arrived from Channapatna that Lutf Ali Beg had been able to dislodge the Marathas and forced them to retreat. But the report did not spark celebrations because Luft Ali's success posed a new problem for Hyder.

While discussing the latest developments with his advisors in his tent, he addressed the tall, broad-chested, curly-haired general, Mohammed Ali, 'God bless Lutf Ali. He has freed Channapatna, but this victory will cause more problems than give us solutions. The retreating Marathas are bound to anger the peshwa who has camped just outside our borders. He might come with his full force and destroy us. We need to stop the peshwa at any cost.'

Mohammed Ali asked, 'What do you propose we do?'

'He has not had much success in this campaign. We need to offer him a way to save his face so that he doesn't take any drastic action after the failure of his forces at Channapatna.' He turned to Khande Rao and commanded, 'Go to the peshwa's camp as our ambassador. Convey to them that we are ready to pay the chauth. We haven't paid them tributes for some time now. I hope this gesture pacifies the peshwa.'

Khande Rao was given some gold and precious stones to be offered as gifts to the peshwa. He left for the peshwa's camp in haste and was back within a matter of days. Greeting Hyder in his tent, Khande Rao said, 'My lord, the peshwa has demanded a tribute of thirty-six lakh rupees. If we pay him, he will cease this campaign and withdraw to Poona.'

A surprised Hyder said, 'I don't have that kind of money, and you already know that, Khande Rao.'

'Yes, my lord, I am well aware of the situation. I have been able to negotiate a deal whereby you will pay fifteen lakhs now, while the rest can be remitted later. The Maratha bankers have agreed to accept your personal guarantee in lieu of the remaining amount for now. You already have fifteen lakhs. We can pay the peshwa immediately and end this campaign on a winning note for everybody.'

Hyder was impressed with Khande Rao's negotiation skills. He had averted a potential military disaster. 'Well done, Khande Rao,' he said. 'Make the necessary arrangements for the payment. Let's survive and fight another day.'

Peshwa Madhav Rao, too, was looking for a way out. The politics in Poona required more of his attention than a fight with a vassal here in the south. He accepted the tribute and returned to Poona. Unlike the last time, the Marathas didn't garrison any of the forts. Except for the big cities and major forts, most towns were left to themselves. Hyder quickly occupied all the forts and towns up to Sira and put men loyal to him in charge.

The nizam who, like the peshwa, considered Mysore his feudatory and was closely observing the situation, decided to make his move once the Marathas left the scene. After their exit, the province of Sira, or whatever was left of it, was claimed by the nizam as Mughal land. Despite being renegades themselves, the nizam had no qualms about invoking the name of the Mughals to annex territories. But at the same time, he had his hands full with the court intrigues in Hyderabad and was not in a position to deploy his army to annex Sira. So, he ordered Hyder to capture Sira in the name of the nizam.

This was an opportunity for Hyder to legitimately take control of Sira. He gathered the forces which were already deployed in the vicinity of Sira and marched towards the fort. The Maratha garrison in Sira was no match for him. Despite being strongly fortified, the precision of the French cannons and the knowledge that no Maratha reinforcements were coming to help made the garrison surrender almost immediately. And so, the fort of Sira was in Hyder's hands for the first time. He filled it with his troops. Taking stock of the situation in Sira, Hyder thought:

I have spent my men and money to conquer Sira. I will no longer waste away my life running and hiding and bowing down to the Marathas and the nizam. This ends today. I need to stand up to them. Sira is mine. After all, Mother had told me that my father died defending this fort against the nizam. I will not do justice to my ancestors if I hand over Sira to the nizam.

He had decided that Sira was his and if the nizam thought otherwise, he would have to fight for it. However, the nizam was thinking in a completely different direction. He was delighted that Sira was now part of his empire, and he bestowed on Hyder the title of Nawab Hyder Ali Khan to honour his accomplishments. Hyder Ali was now officially an Indian prince.

Sira, a provincial Mughal capital, was grandly designed, towering over other capital cities in the region. For the first time, Hyder stepped into the city his father had once pledged allegiance to and eventually sacrificed his life for. It was a bittersweet experience for Hyder: he had conquered the place that had nourished and yet taken his father away from him. He was now the ruler of the entire Sira province. The first thing he did upon his arrival was to visit his father's grave. His face was still and impassive as he sought his father's blessings.

I don't remember anything about my father. My mother was everything to me. And then Shahbaz and now the only person I look up to is Diwan Nanjaraja. Mother loved my father a lot. Even decades after his death, she cried thinking of him. He must have been a good man. I must pay my respects to the man she had loved so dearly.

He then moved around and explored the city that was his now and was spellbound by the sheer grandeur he witnessed. Even though it was clearly in decline, Sira was still more magnificent than Srirangapatna or even Arcot. The mosque built by Aurangzeb was a beautiful sight and the Mughal gardens left a lasting impression on Hyder.

When his court was in session in the palace, he said, 'Wouldn't it be lovely to have such gardens back home? They are so soothing. Order the engineers to build a similar garden in Bangalore. Let's call it by the same name – Lalbagh, a garden filled with red roses.'

Hyder's courtiers wrote down the orders as he continued listing his desires. 'I would also like to build a palace like this one for me and my family in Bangalore. Khande Rao, lead this endeavour and make sure the finances are in order for the completion of this new building.'

These were good times for Hyder, a period of enjoyment after a long and arduous campaign. Over the next four years, he spent more and more time administering the various districts of Mysore and filling up the treasury through his robust revenue mechanisms. With Khande Rao's assistance and guidance, he was turning Mysore into an economic powerhouse. Despite being deeply involved in civil activities, he did not forget his military ambitions. He went on a hiring spree, recruiting French engineers and mercenaries. His generals Lutf Ali Beg and Mohammed Ali were encouraged by him to modernize the army. Hyder was slowly transforming his army into one of the most lethal forces in India.

With the thriving economy and no wars in sight, Nawab Hyder Ali was able to provide a comfortable life to his family. During these years of prosperity, he and Fatima were also blessed with another son, Karim, and a daughter, Majeeda. Things were almost perfect in Mysore.

The winter of 1759, Srirangapatna

In the late hours of the night, Khande Rao was in a secret meeting with the Queen Mother at Krishnaraja Wodeyar's palace in Srirangapatna.

'The diwan is at his weakest now. Now is the time to act, my queen, for the betterment of all of us.'

'These are times of peace, Khande. We must have a strong reason for making changes in the administration. Nanjaraja has anyway become weak, confining himself to Srirangapatna and regretting the death of his brother every day. There is no need to replace him,' the Queen Mother replied.

'Have you forgotten the murder of your first son? Devaraja and Nanjaraja are different sides of the same coin. Our diwan will not hesitate to kill your other son either. I recommend that you replace him with someone loyal to you and the king. Having me as your diwan will finally put the power of the Mysore kingdom back in the rightful hands of our king, Krishnaraja Wodeyar.'

'It will not be that easy to dislodge Nanjaraja. He still controls a strong army and the capital.'

'My queen, the diwan is not as strong as before. He has become old and his thinking has also weakened. None of his personal troops guard the Srirangapatna fort or any of the other cities. His influence doesn't extend beyond his palace. Yet, Mysore answers to him and the diwan still sees our king merely as a figurehead. It is not right for our king to be a mere puppet. Mysore belongs to him, and it is our duty to have him rule the kingdom unchallenged as desired by you, the people of Mysore – and by God!'

'I don't know, Khande. I fear for Krishnaraja's life. Nanjaraja is a cruel man and would not hesitate to murder my son. My son's life is more important than who gets to control Mysore.'

'If we want our king to be safe then the diwan must go – that is the only solution. We need to address the root of the problem, and that is Nanjaraja.'

The Queen Mother finally gave in to Khande Rao's dangerous suggestion. She said, 'I will counsel the king. I hope you are right, Khande. I am playing with my son's life here.'

'There is nothing to worry about, my queen. Everything will go as per our plan.'

Nanjaraja was fast asleep when his personal retainer woke him up. Nanjaraja's power had been, by now, reduced to only the administration of Srirangapatna. In fact, he had even relinquished control of the daily administration of the capital to men loyal to him. His daily interactions with officials had reduced drastically. He was not the Nanjaraja of old. He had lost the heart and zeal to either collect money or occupy more land. So when the retainer woke him up in the afternoon to deliver an important message, Nanjaraja did not particularly care for it, but that changed soon.

'My lord, the king has passed an order this afternoon which will interest you.' The retainer passed a piece of paper to his master.

Nanjaraja read the paper and anger clouded his face, but he soon calmed down. The king had issued a proclamation that Khande Rao would replace Nanjaraja as the diwan of Mysore state. The dispossessed diwan no longer had the energy to take on the king. He had one regret though. He should have killed the king, but it was too late now.

Hyder came to Nanjaraja's palace later in the evening. 'I presume you have received the order, my lord.'

'You were part of this, Hyder?'

'Khande Rao told me about the order yesterday. He told me that the king and the Queen Mother were keen on passing this order. They asked for my approval, which I gave.'

'Do you know what they are trying to do to me?'

'My lord, I approved the decision, keeping your interest in mind. The ravages of war and the court have taken a toll on you. You are not the same anymore. I think you should rest.'

'Yes, I do need rest, but I wanted to make that decision myself.'

'You can still continue as diwan, my lord. It's your decision and not the king's. But personally, I feel the order issued by the king is for your own good, my lord. You need some respite.'

'Do you really think the king made this decision on his own?'

'I know it is not the king's decision. I will have a word with Khande Rao. I have been receiving information about him acting out of turn for some time now.'

Nanjaraja gave a tired smile. 'Keep your enemies closer, Hyder. Anyway, I have decided to retire. I don't think I can fight the tide that has risen against me now.'

'Please let me know if I can help with anything.'

'You are already forcing me out, Hyder. What help can I seek from you?' Nanjaraja asked with a rueful smile.

Preparations for Nanjaraja's departure were underway. He had submitted to the king's proclamation and did not lead any rebellion in the capital. He wanted to retreat to his jagir, a large tract that was bestowed by the king's ancestors to his family, and lead a peaceful retired life. But a problem was brewing in the Queen Mother's quarters.

'My queen, how can I be diwan if I don't have the *sunnad* for the *diwangiri*?' Khande Rao asked.

'We will make them for you, Khande. A piece of paper doesn't give you legitimacy – it is our word that gives you the right,' the queen tried to pacify him.

'But my queen, Nanjaraja may not agree with you. He still holds the papers of appointment, the sunnad of your ancestors. He can claim the diwangiri any time he wants. A lot of palegars still swear loyalty to him. He has a large personal treasury, a large jagir and strong private army. He is still powerful enough to claim it.'

'Khande, we will pass an order rescinding the old order. You are needlessly worrying about some piece of paper instead of preparing for your new role.'

'My queen, we both know of the treachery that Nanjaraja is capable of. As long as the papers are with him, he is a threat to the king, and to Mysore. We need to retrieve the papers from him for the good of our state.'

The Queen Mother sighed and asked, 'How do you propose we ask him to give up the papers?'

'Send a strongly worded letter to him. If he refuses, don't honour the jagir rights bestowed on him.'

'Khande, he has his own army. I don't think a strongly worded letter would work.'

Khande Rao was silent for a while, and after a few minutes, he said, 'Why don't you ask the dalwai to ask him? He is the most powerful man in Mysore and Nanjaraja likes him. He will be able to convince Nanjaraja.'

Heeding Khande Rao's advice, the Queen Mother summoned Hyder to her palace. 'Nawab Hyder Ali, we need the sunnad for the diwangiri from Nanjaraja. I would like you to procure the papers for us.'

'Papers?' Hyder asked.

'Yes. Our ancestors have accorded the rights of the diwangiri to Nanjaraja's ancestors, which were passed on to Devaraja and then to Nanjaraja. We need those papers to pass on the responsibilities to Khande Rao.'

Khande Rao, who was standing next to the Queen Mother, nodded in agreement. Hyder looked at him, 'Papers don't make a diwan. This is not an issue at all. The diwan has agreed to relinquish the post, and I believe that is more than enough.'

'We would like to honour our traditions. Therefore, I request you to procure the papers. Since Nanjaraja has already relinquished power, he should have no qualms about giving you the papers.'

Hyder saw the pointlessness in the conversation and decided that it was better to ask Nanjaraja for the papers. He had never been given any papers that certified his dalwaigiri, and yet he was recognized as the dalwai. Believing it to only be a small hassle for Nanjaraja, Hyder headed to his mentor's palace. But the soldiers outside refused to allow him entry.

What has happened to Nanjaraja? Has he flown into one of his fits of anger again? He had surely calmed down. Why is he not cooperating with me now?

Hyder's thoughts were interrupted when the soldiers in Nanjaraja's palace fired a cannon at his entourage. Luckily, the shot missed him and he retreated immediately. But he was back soon and surrounded the palace with his army. Then he sent a message asking Nanjaraja to explain the reason behind this display of hostility. The reply was more cannon fire. Hyder decided to end the stand-off and had some of his best troops scale the walls of the palace and sabotage the cannons. With the cannons out of the way, his foot soldiers went through the gates, dodging musket fire, and subdued all the soldiers loyal to Nanjaraja.

Hyder didn't bother to go inside. He ordered one of his lieutenants to confiscate the papers and send Nanjaraja to his jagir at the earliest. What he didn't know was that Khande Rao had already sent a notice asking Nanjaraja to hand over the papers, even before Hyder had agreed to talk to Nanjaraja. This arrogant demand had angered Nanjaraja, and he had assumed that Hyder was also part of the plot to dispose of him. So, when his protégé came over to his palace, he had ordered his men to fire the cannons at him. But Hyder Ali was the strongest man in the land, and Nanjaraja's handful of troops were no match for his army. As ordered by the dalwai, Nanjaraja was quickly bundled off to his jagir, quite far away from Srirangapatna.

Hyder summoned Khande Rao to his palace that night. The ever-subservient Khande Rao quickly arrived. 'Don't think that I don't know what happened today, Khande Rao. Don't you dare do things behind my back again,' warned Hyder.

To Hyder's surprise, Khande Rao's submissiveness vanished, and he looked at his master straight in the eye. But Hyder continued, 'Remember this: every action that you take as diwan needs to be approved by me. You work for me. Being the diwan doesn't make you the overlord of Mysore. I'm watching you.'

Khande Rao showed no fear or respect. He had always believed that he was the true power behind the illiterate Hyder Ali. He was sure the success of the dalwai's campaigns was a result of his ingenuity in managing the finances of the kingdom and not the uncouth dalwai running around in the battlefield. He deserved to be more than just an accountant; he deserved to be the diwan – the prime minister of the kingdom. Now that he was finally the Diwan of Mysore, he didn't have to listen to Hyder. The dalwai should be answerable to the diwan and not the other way around. Khande Rao curtly replied, 'Yes, my lord.'

That night, there was another secret meeting in the Queen Mother's palace. Khande Rao was fomenting more trouble: 'The dalwai must go, my queen. Now is the time to act. It is for the good of all of us.'

5

The summer of 1759, Srirangapatna

HYDER ALI HAD POSTED MEN LOYAL TO HIM AT MOST OF the strategic forts and cities in Mysore state. Due to this garrisoning, his standing army was now much smaller. The remaining army, stationed at Srirangapatna, was still formidable. Despite the control he had over Mysore, Hyder's enemies were still alive and kicking. He wanted peace at his borders and to strengthen his hold at the junction where the Nizam and the Nawab of Arcot's territories met adjacent to Mysore's southern borders. For this endeavour, he decided to send his best troops under the command of his most loyal generals to Pondicherry to work out and execute his plan of tightening his hold on the southeast borders of Mysore with the help of the French. With a huge chunk of his army leaving the capital, he barely had 1,000 horsemen and some infantry left. His palace was only protected by a couple of cannons. But he didn't feel the need for more protection. After all, Srirangapatna was a well-guarded city, and it was his home. Nobody from within would attack him, he was certain.

Meanwhile, Khande Rao had been able to convince the Queen Mother, who, in turn, had convinced the king to get rid of Hyder. In this case, a mere proclamation from the king would not work. Hyder had to be removed by force.

Hyder had entrusted most of Srirangapatna's security to Khande Rao. Despite being in charge of the city's defences, Khande Rao didn't want to take any chances. Having established connections with the Marathas while negotiating with them during their last invasion, he decided to leverage his ties with them for his own interests.

Khande Rao sent a secret message to Peshwa Madhav Rao, offering to pay double the chauth if the latter would help him get rid of Hyder. The Peshwa himself had his own grievances against Hyder. The capture of Sira was his biggest grouse, and the fact that the greatest military in India was not able to defeat an upstart pricked him. The lure of additional tribute was just what was needed to start off another Maratha invasion of Mysore.

Rather than following the conventional approach of moving a large army slowly through enemy territory, Madhav Rao chose to have the army split into two contingents, which started moving directly towards Srirangapatna. But they were not fast enough. Hyder had already received word of their impending arrival. However, he was not in a position to put up a strong defence. If it were just the Marathas who had been against him, it would be a different story. But this wasn't the case.

He rushed to his family. 'Wake up! Wake up, Fatima!'

Fatima could barely open her eyes. But seeing her husband in full armour jolted her from her sleep. 'My lord, what is happening? Why are you armoured in the middle of the night?'

'Khande Rao's men have attacked our palace. They have already scaled the walls and will be here in no time.'

Fatima was speechless.

'Take Tipu and go into the inner quarters of the zenana. They will come and take you hostage otherwise. While they search for you, I need to escape from the capital.'

'What? You are leaving us here? I don't understand what's going on.'

'This is the only way I can save you and Tipu. I don't have the time to explain, Begum. Time is of the essence now!'

Not able to fathom the situation, Fatima started crying. Eight-year-old Tipu was brought in by one of the retainers.

Stroking Tipu's head, Hyder told him, 'Son, stay with your mother. I need to leave urgently.'

Tipu was as clueless as his mother. He did not understand why his father was in such a hurry. He only looked at his father with fear in his eyes.

Holding his wife's hand and drawing his son close to him, Hyder said, 'I promise you, I will come back.' Then he rushed out of the zenana. His trusted soldiers, who were waiting outside the zenana, whisked him away.

As they moved out of the ladies' quarters, a soldier informed him, 'The diwan has shut all the gates of the fort, my lord. We will need to scale the walls. The ladders are ready. We will have to take the secret path under the palace that leads to the ladders.'

The group moved swiftly through the dark passages and came out near a wall. Some soldiers were already there, waiting for their leader. One of them said, 'This way, my lord. We will cover your exit.'

Hyder and his aides quickly climbed the ladders and came down the walls on another set of ladders. They rushed to the banks of the Kaveri where some boatmen were huddled together. On seeing Hyder, they quickly untied their *thappa*s, or round bamboo boats, and pushed them onto the water. Horses for the escaping group were also taken across the river. On reaching the opposite bank, Hyder said, 'We are going to Bangalore. My brother-in-law, who is the *khiledar* there, will offer me shelter. Let's move. There's no time to waste.'

The group galloped towards Bangalore in the middle of the night, with almost no stops along the way. Twenty hours later, they were at the gates of the city. These were times when no one could be trusted, and the khiledar of Bangalore did not trust his men either. He was not sure which of them might be spying for Khande Rao. He brought Hyder in through a secret gate. Fortunately for Hyder, the troops in Bangalore were still loyal to him.

Meanwhile, back in Srirangapatna, Khande Rao barged into the zenana to find only Fatima and Tipu.

'Where is Hyder Ali?' he demanded.

By now, Fatima had been informed about Khande Rao's treachery by her aides. On seeing the traitor in the flesh, she struck a defiant note. 'He escaped long ago. What are you going to do about it, you traitor?'

Khande Rao ordered one of his lieutenants, 'They couldn't have gone far. Search the capital. Bring his wife and son and imprison them in the mosque. Watch them round the clock – they will be valuable during our negotiations with Hyder Ali.' He didn't see any need to interrogate Fatima further. His priority was to capture his former master. The mother and son were escorted to the chief mosque in the capital, where they were held captive.

In Bangalore, Hyder had nothing but the men and money of his brother-in-law. All his wealth was in Srirangapatna, which was now under Khande Rao. He needed money to take back his capital and rescue his family. He called on his bankers to raise money to fight against Khande Rao. His good reputation paid off and money poured in from many quarters. Over the course of the next few months he was able to raise a sizeable army. He also sent messages to his army in Pondicherry, asking them to return. But he was running out of time. His contact with the bankers had alerted Khande Rao to his location. And soon, the combined armies of Khande Rao and the Marathas under Peshwa Madhav Rao surrounded Bangalore.

The news of Hyder Ali's larger army moving had reached Khande Rao and the Marathas. The Marathas decided to intercept this army, expecting Khande Rao to continue with the siege of Bangalore. The idea was to take on the split armies of Hyder Ali simultaneously before they combined to become a formidable threat. But the news of the approaching adversaries had rattled Khande Rao. He lost his nerve and retreated from Bangalore to Srirangapatna, fearing an attack by Hyder. The siege on Bangalore was lifted and Hyder was free to move out.

But Hyder's returning army had a tough time dodging the fearsome Marathas. Wave after wave of Maratha cavalry swamped them but the generals held steady, moving their camps night after night and avoiding a direct fight every day. To support his returning army, Hyder opened a new front against the Marathas.

Considering the smaller size of the army he had raised in Bangalore, Hyder adopted guerrilla tactics. He started attacking enemy camps at the most vulnerable times, retreating before they could launch a counter-attack. But neither party really benefited from this strategy. The Marathas were too strong to collapse against this two-front attack and Hyder was too dogged to give up.

Though the battle appeared to be a stalemate, the Marathas still had an upper hand. So, it was a surprise to everyone when Peshwa Madhav Rao called for an emergency war council with Khande Rao.

In the Maratha camp near the ghats south of Srirangapatna, Peshwa Madhav Rao said, 'I need to get back to Poona, Khande Rao. The Afghan king Ahmed Abdali has defeated our forces in Panipat, and we are still counting our losses. I fear the worst. I need to be in Poona and take stock of our mounting losses.'

'But what about me? I can't face Hyder Ali alone. You promised me your support.'

'I will leave enough troops here for you to lead and defeat Hyder Ali. But let me leave now because I must be in Poona in this hour of despair.'

Khande Rao had never led an army. The peshwa had been his strength. If the peshwa left him alone on the field, he was not sure he could defeat Hyder Ali. He had to convince the peshwa to stay back. 'Is there no honour in the peshwa's word? I have staked my life for you to bring Mysore under your control. We are almost there, we have cornered Hyder Ali. This is a rare opportunity to vanquish him. You need to honour your promise and help me defeat this man.'

'You have given me everything? You ran away from Bangalore when I went to intercept Hyder Ali's army. You didn't come to fight when he attacked me from behind. I have lost my army and family to the Afghans. I have thousands of widows to console at home, and yet I am here. You dare talk of my honour? It is because of the honour of the peshwa that I am leaving a large army here. Don't you dare question me again!' Madhav Rao raged.

The peshwa and his generals left Mysore, leaving Khande Rao with two large Maratha contingents. But the tables had turned. Hyder's army had regrouped and was marching against his former accountant.

Not only did Khande Rao not have any real battle experience, he was also not a brave man. Rather than fighting Hyder, he slowly started retreating towards Srirangapatna. But Hyder was catching up with him, and Khande Rao was finally forced to face him at Nanjangud.

Hyder started off with precise firing at Khande Rao's camp with his cannons. But the Maratha cavalry formed strong flanks around Khande Rao's army, and despite the fire from the cannons, Khande Rao felt quite safe. Hyder then sent across his kuzzaks to harass the Maratha cavalry and wean them away from the flanks. But Khande Rao made his personal safety a priority and didn't allow the cavalry to move away, despite the constant attacks from the kuzzaks. Seeing that there was no progress, Hyder decided to withdraw his forces. Khande Rao had won for the day.

Back in the camp, Hyder pondered over his strategy.

I don't have the numbers to take on Khande Rao. The Maratha forces protect him and are a constant threat. I need more troops to match him. But I can't withdraw troops from the forts and cities that I control because Khande Rao is sure to occupy them otherwise. Without additional troops, I will not be able to vanquish the traitor. But where can I get additional troops?

His thoughts drifted to his mentor.

I need to meet Nanjaraja. He is my only hope.

Hyder and a few of his trusted aides travelled to Nanjaraja's jagir. They weren't expecting a welcome, let alone a warm one. But Nanjaraja showed none of his previous anger. He even allowed the men into his personal quarters.

Hyder was the first one to speak. 'I am sorry, my lord. I did not foresee this situation for you.'

'Forcing me into retirement is one thing but attacking my palace and bundling me out is another. You betrayed me, Hyder.'

'I attacked the palace only in self-defence. Your cannons nearly killed me. Scaling your palace was a decision taken in the spur of the moment. I never wanted to harm you. I would never do that.'

'But you were willing to threaten me with the loss of my jagir if I didn't hand over the sunnad.'

'I didn't have anything to do with that. In fact, I made sure you got your jagir after you left the capital. It must have been Khande Rao. Only he can think of such base tricks.'

If there was one person Nanjaraja had ever loved, it was Hyder. He had looked at him as his son, his successor. Nanjaraja had no qualms about giving up the diwangiri of Mysore, but what hurt him the most was Hyder betraying him and attacking him in his own palace. Still, deep inside his heart, his love for Hyder was alive. Just one sentence from Hyder claiming innocence was enough for Nanjaraja to forgive him.

There was relief on Nanjaraja's face. 'I knew you wouldn't do such a vile thing. But you still didn't support me in my hour of need. Why, Hyder?'

'My lord, I thought it was in your best interest to retire to your jagir. I really felt you needed some rest.'

Nanjaraja had always cared about Hyder. He merely needed a reason to restore his faith in him. 'Well, it is good to have you back, son.'

'I need your assistance, my lord. Khande Rao attacked me in the middle of the night, and I barely escaped from Srirangapatna. He has sought the support of the Marathas who had me pinned down until now. When the Afghans defeated the Marathas near Panipat, the Peshwa sped back to Poona. But they have left strong contingents to help Khande Rao – it is still difficult to defeat him on the battlefield. I need your assistance.'

'But how can an old man help you?'

Hyder was silent. He wanted Nanjaraja's troops and palegars to come to his aid. But he couldn't force the words out.

'Your tongue is tangled, son? Never mind, I know what you want and I am ready to give it to you. I will have the palegars who are loyal to me provide you with supplies and shelter. My troops are at your disposal.'

Hyder knew Nanjaraja's troops and supplies wouldn't be enough. But his shame and regret about abandoning his old master prevented him from speaking up. He didn't have the courage to ask Nanjaraja. He remained silent, his eyes lowered.

Nanjaraja knew what was going through Hyder's mind. He said, 'Along with my troops, I will support you in your quest to recover Srirangapatna. I will officially declare my support to you so that my loyalists fight under your banner. I am old now, Hyder. I can't be with you in person, but I am with you in spirit.'

Hyder smiled, 'Thank you, my lord.' He had won back his mentor's trust.

6

The summer of 1761, Srirangapatna

HYDER WAS ABLE TO MUSTER SOME MORE SOLDIERS AND procure ammunition and cannons from the local chieftains. It was time for another battle with Khande Rao. He got his troops together and started to march towards Srirangapatna once more. Khande Rao hadn't yet reached the capital. He had gained enough confidence after the last battle and decided to face Hyder's army.

Hyder's strategy would be no different from last time. He would attack the middle of the army with the cannons while harassing the flanks with his light cavalry. The only change was that he had more cannons for the middle and many more horses for the flanks.

The cannonade started briskly and the kuzzaks moved against the flanks at lightning speed. Two years later, the Maratha flanks were not as steady as before. The sheer number of kuzzaks meant that the Maratha cavalry had to break formation to fend them off. But the middle suffered the biggest impact. Some of the cannon shots landed very close to the cavalry guarding Khande Rao. An experienced general would have held his troops in formation despite the shock of an intense cannonade, but Khande Rao was neither a war veteran nor an experienced general. He lost his nerve in the face of the crisis and bolted to Srirangapatna, yet again, leaving his army and everything else behind. Seeing their leader in flight, his army soon lost courage and retreated with their general, as the whole formation collapsed. The Maratha cavalry, harassed and having lost formation, had nothing to protect. So, they too retreated to Srirangapatna.

This was a major victory for Hyder. He couldn't capture Khande Rao, but he had him holed up in Srirangapatna. But his own family was being held hostage within the fort. This was a delicate situation and the next steps would have to be taken carefully. Hyder called in Lutf Ali Beg to discuss their next course of action.

Lutf Ali started with a proposal: 'We need to eliminate the Maratha cavalry before making any decisive moves.'

'Yes, I agree. But we must also be careful with our approach. If we push Khande Rao too far and too soon, I will be putting my family's lives in danger. We need a subtle approach.'

'What do you propose we do?'

Hyder deliberated on this some more.

Khande Rao knows that there will be a blockade, if not a siege, at Srirangapatna. His calculations would be based on this assumption. His greatest strength is his Maratha contingent. The focus needs to be on neutralizing the most significant threat in the most discreet manner to avoid an escalation by Khande Rao, which may result in him harming my family.

He kept thinking about every possibility and its consequences until he finally had a brainwave. 'Nanjaraja still has good relations with the Marathas, especially with the two generals with Khande Rao, and he knows this. We must forge a couple of letters addressed to the Maratha generals from Nanjaraja. The letters must demand the arrest of Khande Rao, as discussed in a secret meeting between Nanjaraja and the Maratha generals. These letters must find their way to Khande Rao. This will sow the seeds of doubt and paranoia in his mind. Prepare the letters and send a trusted man into Srirangapatna right away. Ensure that he is caught and the letters reach Khande Rao.'

This elaborate plan was executed perfectly. The letters made their way to Khande Rao and, as expected, paranoia took hold of him. Before he could take any action, the Maratha generals, fearing for their lives, decided it was best to abandon him and leave Srirangapatna. Almost the entire Maratha cavalry in the city slipped away and moved towards Poona.

Hyder quickly ordered his kuzzaks to harass the Marathas constantly and direct their path into an ambush. The kuzzaks moved along with the Maratha cavalry and forced them into uneven terrain, which made it difficult for the horses to move. It was a shallow valley and Hyder had already set up his cannons at the top. As soon as the entire cavalry was inside the valley, he opened fire. Many Marathas were killed and before it turned into a rout, the rest of them surrendered. Hyder confiscated their horses, supplies and money before letting them go. He didn't have time for taking in prisoners. He needed to go back to Srirangapatna and meet Khande Rao one last time.

Hyder and his army camped near the Srirangapatna fort. Lutf Ali Beg was impatient. He said, 'We need to lay siege to the fort before Khande Rao escapes.'

'If we lay siege, he will immediately lay his hands on my family. We need a quick solution and I know exactly what to do.' There was a sparkle in Hyder's eyes. 'Have all our cannons moved to the eastern end of the fort. I want all of them to target the zenana of our king, Krishnaraja. We will have the king open the gates for us.'

It was a quiet, dry afternoon in Srirangapatna. The silence was broken by a loud blast from Hyder's camp. Cannonballs started raining on the king's palace, which was sheltered away from the fort wall. The French engineers and their cannons were extremely accurate and the walls of the palace began to crumble.

Khande Rao had at least sat on a horse to lead an army on the field. Krishnaraja Wodeyar had virtually been a prisoner for most of his life under the brothers Devaraja and Nanjaraja. After the brothers' loss of power, he had stayed in the palace while Khande Rao battled Hyder Ali. The Mysore king had no battle experience. The firing continued until daybreak, but the king's courage didn't last the night. A messenger was sent to Hyder the next morning imploring for peace and inviting him inside the fort.

Inside his tent, the letter sent by the king was read out to Hyder. He said, 'Well, the fort is ours but that is not enough.' He called his scribe and said, 'Write a letter stating that Khande Rao must be handed over to me, and my troops must be allowed free passage into the fort with absolutely no restrictions. In return, I will spare the lives of the king and his family, and Mysore will still be ruled in the name of the king.'

The writer promptly drafted the message and gave it to the king's messenger who took it back to the king. The king's council was inexperienced in both negotiations and diplomacy. They saw no option other than to agree to Hyder's proposal.

The victorious army entered the fort and scaled all the towers and walls. When Hyder entered Srirangapatna, he immediately rushed to the city's main mosque. His soldiers had already taken over the building and were guarding the entrance to the mosque. They ushered him inside. Standing in the courtyard were Fatima and Tipu. There was nobody else. On seeing Hyder, Tipu ran towards him.

Hoisting his son up, Hyder said, 'My child, it is good to see that you are safe. Didn't I promise that I will return for you?'

Tipu was glad that his father was back. He held on tightly to his father as Hyder walked towards Fatima. Fatima's eyes had welled up but there was relief in them too. It had been months since Hyder had seen his wife and son.

'I am sorry that I had to leave you and Tipu behind. I spent every waking moment outside, only thinking of the two of you. I did everything under my control to rescue you and now I am finally here. We are safe.'

Fatima didn't reply. She moved forward and hugged Hyder tightly. The family was united again.

The guards took the family back to their palace. With his family safe, Hyder went to the king's palace. It was already late in the night but the royal family was asked to grant an audience to Hyder, who was informed that Khande Rao would also be with the king.

Hyder entered the durbar to find the king sitting on the throne, the Queen Mother to his right on a chair and Khande Rao standing behind her, his face frozen in fear.

The sombre Queen Mother addressed the dalwai, 'Nawab Hyder Ali, thank you for ceasing the attack. The king has kept his word. Your soldiers now guard Srirangapatna. Khande Rao is here as well.' She continued, 'The king has held his side of the bargain but I want you to promise me something. You will not kill Khande Rao. You will not torture him either. He made a foolish decision, and you should not punish him with death.'

Hyder looked at Khande Rao and a smile broke on his face. Calmy, he replied, 'My queen, thank you for keeping your word. Srirangapatna has got its rightful dalwai back, and I will serve the king as before. I understand your concern about Khande Rao's fate. I have immense respect for your request and I assure you I will treat him the way I treat my pet parrot. That's my promise.'

And so, Khande Rao was handed over to Hyder. He ordered the accountant to be taken to Bangalore. With the meeting over, Hyder looked at the king and his mother and mused: *I trusted these people but they had shattered that trust. I need to safeguard my interests. Otherwise, I will be risking the lives of Fatima and Tipu. I can't let that happen again. I need to keep the royal family under control.*

Exiting the palace, he ordered his generals to confine the movement of the king and the Queen Mother to the palace.

The Mysore royalty had sought to become more independent with the help of Khande Rao but in the end, their freedoms were curtailed even further. They were now not allowed to move freely out of their palace and their messages were regularly intercepted by Hyder Ali's men.

With Srirangapatna safe in his hands, Hyder went to Bangalore to decide Khande Rao's fate. Once inside the Bangalore Fort, he ordered Khande Rao to be brought to court. Khande Rao did not believe that Hyder would keep his promise. The fear of death was visible on his face.

'Well, Khande Rao, we meet again,' Hyder greeted him with a wry smile.

The prisoner trembled with fear as he looked up to the master of his fate.

'I am a man of my word,' said Hyder. 'I will keep my promise to the Queen Mother. I will indeed treat you like I treat my pet parrot. Have you seen my parrot?'

Hyder looked around. 'Bring me my parrot,' he said to one of his retainers.

Within minutes, the parrot was brought into the court.

'Look at my pretty green parrot. It's so happy inside its iron cage. Chirping all day. It is kept inside the palace and it is given good care. It is fed well – a bowl of rice every day. As I promised the Queen Mother, you will receive the same care. You will be one of the luckiest parrots in Mysore.'

The smile on Hyder's face vanished and was replaced with rage.

'Put him in an iron cage!' he ordered his men. 'Feed him from the same bowl of rice from now on.'

An iron cage was brought into the court. A couple of soldiers came forward, stripped Khande Rao and threw him into the cage. The cage was dragged away, with the prisoner wailing for mercy. In a month's time, he had starved to death in the iron cage.

Hyder's retribution was not yet complete. Quite a few palegars had sided with Khande Rao, and it was time for them to pay the price. Each of them was ordered to either pay a huge war indemnity or face execution. Over the next few months, they were systematically punished for their betrayal.

After a fair amount of warfare over many months, Hyder was going through the list of palegars who were yet to be punished. As his writer was going through the names in the Nawab of Mysore's court, Hyder asked him to stop at one particular name. It was the palegar of Doddaballapur.

Closing his eyes, Hyder smiled to himself. 'I know Kuli Khan. He will learn how the wheel of time turns when we visit him.'

The forces of retribution marched towards Doddaballapur. Kuli Khan had not forgotten Hyder Ali. Nor had he forgotten the torture he had meted out to the nawab. Fearing for his life, he fled to Arcot with his family. Hyder was welcomed to a town with no ruler.

One of his generals offered, 'Kuli Khan has escaped to Arcot. With your permission, we will bring him back.'

Hyder smiled, 'He is an old man now, practically harmless. He has left his entire jagir for me. Why should I go chasing after him? He will live in fear for the rest of his life, and that's a good enough punishment.'

The Khande Rao affair had brought Mysore under Hyder's control. His loyalists occupied all the important civil positions across the kingdom; the bankers, merchants and traders stood by his side and the Mysore army answered to him.

The diplomats and the ruling class of the Marathas and the nizam may have addressed him as their nawab in their letters but in reality, they shared the same opinion as the citizens of Mysore: Hyder Ali was now practically the Sultan of Mysore. But he would always laugh off such suggestions and reiterate that he was merely a servant of the king of Mysore.

With no more immediate warfare in sight, Hyder once more turned his attention to administration and fixed the revenues of the state. The state of Mysore grew prosperous and wealthy under his able governance. Its borders expanded further, subsuming the erstwhile Sira province, parts of the Arcot province and all the feudatories of the old Mysore kingdom. Hyder Ali was now one of the pre-eminent rulers of south India.

The summer of 1762, Srirangapatna

After spending eight months scouring Mysore, eliminating all those who stood against him, there was finally peace in the kingdom. Hyder yearned for the presence of his son and his wife. It was time to return home, to his family.

Soon, Hyder was back in Srirangapatna and talking to the maulvis in his court. 'I don't want my son to be like me. I am illiterate – my uncle didn't bother to educate me. He wanted a soldier and he got one. Tipu is the son of a nawab, and he needs an education befitting the son of a nawab. I want my son to be a man of culture, not just a soldier.'

A maulvi answered the nawab, 'Tipu can get a good education at Gurramkonda, his maternal grandfather's home. There are excellent teachers there. He will emerge a completely rounded man as he will also receive his military training with Lutf Ali Beg there. He will be ready to be a fine heir to you, my lord.'

The old Lutf Ali Beg was also at the court. He said, 'Your family will be safe in Gurramkonda. Also, I will put some troops there as a buffer against the machinations of the Nawab of Kadapa.'

The other generals in the court nodded in agreement.

Tipu must get the best that is available. I need to provide him with all that I never got in my life. I want him to be a refined noble rather than a coarse general like me. Even if it means my son and I have to be apart.

Hyder spoke, 'It's decided then. Prepare for the journey to Gurramkonda. I will personally escort Tipu and my begum to her maternal home.'

Soon after, Hyder went into the zenana to break the news. But the female courtiers had already informed the begum about her husband's decision.

From behind a wooden screen, Fatima said, 'I heard about your decision to send us to my parents' place.'

'Yes, dear. I want the best for our son. I also want him to be with you so that he learns to become a better man.'

'You know he loves you more than he loves me.'

'But you are a better parent than I am. Tipu deserves better than me. You are the right guiding light for him. Besides, this way you will also get to spend time with your parents. You have always asked me to send you to your mother's place. This will be good for you, and Tipu will enjoy their company too.'

Fatima, who had remained hidden behind the screen until this point, came out to face her husband.

'I will miss you,' she said, looking into his eyes.

'We will be together in no time, my love,' he promised.

7

The monsoon of 1763, Srirangapatna

A YOUNG MAN WAITED IMPATIENTLY IN COURT. HE ADDRESSED the minister who had brought him there: 'How long will the proceedings last? He keeps dictating to the writers. When will I get an audience?'

'The nawab is very diligent when it comes to revenue and administration. He keeps everyone on their toes. More than the military, it is his keen eye in these more mundane matters that keeps the empire in one piece. Your turn will come as soon as he is done with the letters and the responses.'

'My problem is bigger than his tangles in revenue. Please get me an audience at the earliest.'

'Patience! I promise you the nawab's complete attention. Please wait for a few more minutes.'

Hyder was blessed with an incredible memory and an observant eye. He single-handedly kept track of the revenue targets, orders given to civil administrators and diplomatic messages from the greater powers of the region. He managed to do all of this while constantly rebuilding his army along European lines and being in constant campaign mode. This meant spending endless hours with his ministers and generals, reading documents and messages sent to him from every nook and corner of the kingdom and dictating orders to his writers to be passed on to the relevant officials. He was in one of those marathon sessions and all minor visitors had to wait until he was done.

While the young man showed signs of fatigue, Hyder was as energetic as ever as the hours passed. Finally, when the administrative matters came to a close, the minister representing the young man came forward and said, 'My lord, the rightful heir of the Bednur kingdom, which lies west of our empire, has come to seek your assistance.'

The young man came forward. He persisted in an impatient tone, 'I am the adopted son of the ruler of Bednur. I was the heir to the throne. With my father's passing, his wife got together with her paramour and took over my kingdom. I tried to resist this coup but they got the better of me. They tried to assassinate me but I managed to escape. Now they think they have got rid of me and are enjoying their ill-gotten powers. I am here to seek your help. Please help me regain my kingdom, and I will pledge my allegiance to you.'

Hyder listened to the young man thoughtfully. 'I will need some time to address your concern. Until then, you are welcome to stay in Srirangapatna as my royal guest.'

Once everyone had left the court, it was time for the spies and intelligence officers to give their reports to Hyder in private. It was this spy network that enabled Hyder to keep an eye on all his personnel and nip any whispers of treason in the bud. The spies submitted their reports, and Hyder in turn gave his orders. Once this was done, he asked some of them to stay back.

'Go to Bednur and find out everything you can about its ruler, economy and military. The boy seems incompetent. I need first-hand information about this kingdom.'

The guest from Bednur enjoyed Hyder's hospitality as the spies scoured his homeland for information. After a few months, they were back with their reports. 'We have not seen a country as rich as Bednur. It is filled with gold, silver, sandal and spices. They control the lands right up to the sea. The weather is pleasant and it feels like paradise on earth. It is also deep inside the forest, hidden from everything nearby.'

'What about the queen?'

'Rani Viramma is a strong woman, and all the citizens have accepted her as the ruler and there is general prosperity in the nation. But their army is no match for your great army, my lord. They are a bunch of brave but undisciplined men.'

'So what is the difficulty in capturing this country?'

'The terrain is treacherous; the rain is unforgiving. It will be altogether a new experience for our army.'

'What about the boy who is with us?'

'He is just another pretender to the throne.'

'Any allies?'

'The country is completely secluded, surrounded by thick forests. They have no contact with other empires.'

'The towns and cities?'

'The towns are separated by forests with no connecting roads. Each town and city can be captured with no reinforcements coming to their aid in time.'

'Good work,' said Hyder, pleased with the reports. 'Go back to Bednur and collect more information about the size of their army and their administration.'

Once his spies left the court, Hyder was alone with his thoughts.

If I can capture Bednur, I should have enough resources to fend off the Marathas and the nizam. At the very least, I will have money to pay their tributes. I should not let go of this opportunity. This is my chance for survival.

The next day, he called a meeting of his generals. 'We will mount a campaign against the kingdom of Bednur. Get the troops and supplies ready. We leave at the earliest.'

Soldiers were asked to return to the barracks. Elephants and horses were assembled. Quartermasters worked with merchants to get supplies into Srirangapatna from far and wide in the Mysore kingdom. Money was procured from bankers to pay for the soldiers and supplies. Scouts were sent ahead to identify the routes that could be taken. The citadel was bustling with activity. Within a couple of months, the army was primed and ready to march. Once Hyder felt that his army was ready, he gave the orders to move out of Srirangapatna.

The troops and supplies started moving west. The dry plains soon gave way to expansive mountains covered with lush green forests. This slowed down the army, and the bullock carts carrying supplies and pulling the cannons struggled to cross the high mountains. There was the bigger danger of the bullocks' legs getting fractured when they made their descent, which had to be even slower than the ascent. The cavalry had to dismount many times and help the infantry cut through the woods to make a path for the slower wagons and carts. There were few places to camp, but not many of any strategic value. It was drudgery all the way.

On the bright side, many small towns and forts along the way fell like ninepins. Either they paid paishkash, a tribute of money, gold and precious stones, to Hyder Ali and escaped his wrath or were slaughtered if they stood against him. Their wooden walls, pikes and rudimentary weapons were no match for the muskets of his army. This region was so backward that they had never seen cavalry before. Hyder's men barely faced any resistance, and soon reached the gates of the Bednur fort and camped near the eastern end.

The Rani of Bednur, Viramma, was alarmed when she saw Hyder Ali's forces outside her capital. She deliberated with her prime minister and her chief general, 'Our small army is no match for the Mysore forces. I don't want a fight. I want peace in our lands. I am pledging my allegiance to the Sultan of Mysore for the safety of my people. Prime Minister, please send our best ambassadors with expensive gifts including gold, sandal and spices, to Hyder's camp. Have them convey our promise of allegiance to them.'

The Prime Minister of Bednur arranged for the gifts to be sent with the ambassadors who then left the fort to visit Hyder's camp.

The ambassadors were welcomed into Hyder's tent, where he held court. They gave bountiful gifts to Hyder and put forward the proposal of their queen.

'My lord, the rani doesn't want a conflict with you. She sees you as the rightful ruler of all lands here, and she is willing to pledge her allegiance to you. She is also ready to give you three lakh rupees every year as tribute and yearly gifts of sandal, spices and exquisite Boohranpur fabrics. She requests you to accept this peace offering and aid in the continued prosperity of Bednur in your name.'

Hyder hadn't come all the way to Bednur to accept a pittance of three lakhs per year. He knew that the riches of Bednur were beyond those of Mysore. If he had access to Bednur, he would have limitless resources to take on the Marathas and the nizam.

'Let me make a proposal in turn. The rani and her family can stay in Srirangapatna as my royal guests with a generous pension in perpetuity. I will take over Bednur and personally manage its affairs.'

The ambassadors were dumbfounded. They were not given an opportunity to negotiate the terms of this new proposal and were asked to return to the fort to deliver Hyder's response.

The rani was calm after hearing the counter-proposal. She said, 'My mind is clear now. I have no other option but to defend my country. Prepare the defences – we are in for a difficult siege.'

On getting no reply from the rani, Hyder ordered the siege batteries to be set up around the fort. Things were not off to a good start. The ground was not flat enough to place the cannons or secure the batteries firmly. This meant that the cannons would not be precise in their aim and the siege batteries didn't offer adequate protection. The terrain itself was not conducive for the famed kuzzaks to attack either. He would now have to rely heavily on his infantry and their muskets.

During a siege, Hyder would usually send the troops not part of the siege to ravage the surrounding lands, thus cutting off all supplies and communications to the besieged fort. This not only depleted the resources of the inhabitants of the fort but also had a huge psychological impact on them, forcing the enemy to surrender. But attacking other towns and settlements in this region was quite a task as there were no roads, and most other towns were quite far away. He was putting his detachments at risk by sending them off to remote locations in a land they hadn't fully explored. But his soldiers were steady and disciplined, and despite the difficult terrain, most towns and settlements were captured. But unlike the forts in the plains, Bednur was well-stocked and self-sufficient. So, Hyder's tactic of forced starvation did not have the desired effect.

Days turned to weeks and weeks turned into months. The detachments sent to capture the neighbouring towns had returned, but there were no signs of surrender from the fort. Despite being imprecise, the cannons pounded the walls of the fort. But the hardy men of Bednur bravely repaired the forts. Scores were killed and maimed by cannon shots during repair work, but new men kept replacing them. The heavy losses did not deter the rani or the citizens of Bednur. She kept the morale of the army high in spite of the barrage of fire and iron from Hyder's forces. The battle was headed towards a stalemate.

8

The winter of 1764, Bednur

IT WAS A LAZY MORNING WHEN THE PERSONNEL MANNING the cannons came out of their tents to resume firing at Bednur's walls. It was by now a futile but routine exercise to fire the cannons from morning until evening or till the ammunition was exhausted. Just like every other morning in the last few months, the personnel got into their positions in the siege battery after having breakfast and were waiting for the order. All of a sudden, horsemen burst out of the thick green forest behind the siege batteries and rushed towards the men, shouting and raising their swords. The men in charge of the cannons froze in fear and surprise. They didn't have any chance to retaliate. The horsemen came in and slew them.

The attacking party also torched the siege battery, which was primarily made of wood. After that, they moved to the next one. The soldiers in the next battery didn't have any muskets with which to defend themselves. The horsemen moved ahead, trampling on the soldiers indiscriminately.

Some of the horsemen were slain by the soldiers but the former were greater in number and in no time they overcame the resistance and torched this battery as well and moved to the others. The destruction was swift and brutal.

Seeing fire and smoke emanating from the siege batteries, the kuzzaks galloped towards the scene. But by then the horsemen had retreated. The damage was done, and quite a few siege batteries had been burnt. There was chaos everywhere, with dead and wounded soldiers strewn all around the burning structures.

It was late evening before order was restored. A livid Hyder called for a war council meeting that night.

General Mohammed Ali, who led the kuzzaks, made the first comments. 'The Pathans of Savanur attacked us this morning, burning five of our siege batteries and killing hundreds of our soldiers. By the time our cavalry could react, they had already retreated. We couldn't pursue them because of the challenging and unknown terrain. But, they seem to know the terrain well and were able to evade us. All five cannons from the burnt siege batteries have been salvaged. With a few repairs by the French engineers, we will have them firing again.'

A visibly angry Hyder asked, 'How have our spies failed us like this? How did none of you know that the Nawab of Savanur was supporting the rani? I was told that she had no support. None of your scouts told me about the Afghan-Pathan cavalry.'

General Mohammed Ali replied, 'Our apologies, my lord. We will not let this happen again.'

Hyder didn't like the answer. He flared up, 'What do you mean it will not happen again? Will that bring back my dead soldiers?'

The general kept his head down.

Hyder regained his composure. 'I can't worry about your mistakes right now. We need to secure ourselves against the next wave of attacks.'

He looked at General Mohammed Ali for answers. The general replied, 'I would recommend increased security at each battery and having our infantry guard the outer perimeter of the siege batteries. That way, we will be secure against any outside attacks. The kuzzaks would be on standby as a quick reaction force to purse any potential attackers.'

'This would mean having more of my troops put into active service now. We can't sustain heightened alertness for long durations especially in a siege like this, Mohammed Ali.'

'My lord, we need to survive today to fight tomorrow. I would recommend these temporary measures until we vanquish the Pathans.'

Despite his anger at the failure of his men, he trusted them to rectify their wrongs and come out on top against the new adversary. Hyder yielded to General Mohammed Ali's suggestion.

After a detailed discussion on the proposal, more troops were assigned to man the siege batteries and the infantry was put into an active formation to protect the equipment. There was no activity for the next few days, but everyone was alert.

Late one night, spies and scouts reached Hyder's tent. 'We are expecting an attack from the Afghans tomorrow. We have been tracking their movement in the forest. They are quite close and will most likely descend on us soon.'

Thanks to this intelligence, Hyder was prepared.

It was yet another foggy morning, but the infantry was ready. The Pathan horsemen, not knowing that they were expected, began the climb up the hill to reach the Mysore camp. In order to move discreetly, they climbed at a slow pace. As they drew near the camp, a volley of fire was sent in their direction. Many horses and men fell to the attack. The whole place was choked with smoke and the smell of gunpowder. But the Pathans didn't give up. They galloped towards the muskets in a frenzy.

There was another volley of fire, and more Pathan horsemen were killed but they still wouldn't stop or even slow down. The remaining horses kept moving up when, all of a sudden, the kuzzaks came hurtling down, slashing at every Pathan horseman along the way. None of them survived; their bodies lay scattered all over the hill, soaked in red from the blood of the Afghans which was now being washed away by the rain.

The monsoon had arrived.

The rains in this region were harsh. It poured and poured; the ground became a slushy mess, making the upkeep of the siege batteries even harder. Diseases started spreading through the camp but Hyder did not yield. He wanted Bednur, and no rain or torrent could stop him. He persisted with the cannonade, his ammunition constantly damaging the fort walls and killing anybody who arrived to repair the walls.

The siege had now been active for one year, and Hyder's anger knew no bounds. 'I refuse to accept this defeat! I don't care if I lose more men. We will storm the fort. Prepare the army and scale the walls. We will not retreat!'

He soon got the entire infantry prepared for a direct assault on the fort. It was a desperate situation for him, a huge gamble. To improve the morale of the soldiers, he made a generous proposition. 'Once the fort is captured, all the soldiers will be allowed to loot and plunder anything they want for an entire day. Rani Viramma will feel the full wrath of my army.'

When the news of Hyder's permission to loot and plunder reached the soldiers, it raised their spirits. Such was the allure for plunder that even the cavalrymen got off their horses and prepared to scale the walls to be a part of the upcoming attack. There was a newfound zeal in the eyes of the soldiers. Bednur was about to experience hell.

Ladders were placed against the walls of the fort. Bednur soldiers tried toppling the ladders and slashing and killing anyone who made it to the top. But the sheer number of Mysore soldiers, multiple ladders and the speed of the soldiers climbing up ensured that the brave Bednur soldiers were overwhelmed. The fight continued on the fort walls.

In the midst of the raging fight, the Bednur general ran towards the large wooden palace that was in the middle of the fort. He raced up the stairs and entered the court.

Rani Viramma was at the far end of the court with her personal bodyguards. A lady of medium height and slim build, her face exuded majesty and confidence. She was dressed for battle and the guards were putting the last pieces of armour on her. As a guard adjusted the metal headgear on her head, she saw her general enter the court.

'My queen, Hyder Ali's soldiers have scaled the walls of the fort. Our soldiers are putting their lives at stake trying to stop them, but they are too many. The rumour is that Hyder Ali has allowed them to plunder our city if it is captured.'

Gripping the sword handed to her by her guard, she commanded, 'Defend your home. We will not surrender. We will fight till our last breath.'

A concerned look appeared on the general's face. It was almost as if he could see the future and was trying his best to avoid the fate that the queen's words would hurl him and his beloved Bednur into.

'My queen, we will not let the honour of Bednur down. But you will have to leave the fort. I am afraid that they will try to violate you once they are inside. Your honour is sacred to us. Please take the secret path and escape while we defend your exit.'

Rani Viramma was livid on hearing her general's words. She roared back at him, 'Leave now? Never! I am responsible for my people's safety. I would rather die here, fighting for Bednur, than escape.'

'I implore you, my queen. Your life and honour are paramount to us. I beg you to leave through the secret passageway. I promise you we will not let anyone tarnish the name of Bednur.'

Just then, the prime minister entered the court. He was out of breath. Addressing the rani, he said, 'My queen, the fort walls have been taken over by Hyder Ali's forces. They are making their way into the palace. Our soldiers are stalling their progress, but they are too many and they are forcing their way through.'

The general got down on his knees, 'I beg you, my queen. Please leave now.'

The prime minister grasped the situation immediately. He concurred with the general, 'We need you alive, my queen. We need you to lead the resistance against Mysore. The fort may be lost today, but we will definitely win it back in the future, and we need your guidance in taking our Bednur back. We need you, my queen. We need you to survive this hour of darkness.'

The rani reluctantly agreed with her prime minister. A few slave girls were chosen to accompany her. They made their way out of the palace through a secret passageway. Within a few minutes, she was outside. As they ran towards the hidden pathway that led to the fort walls, Rani Viramma stopped and turned around for one last look at her home.

The palace was decorated with bright red Chinese tiles and adorned with exquisite sandalwood figurines. The teak pillars with their delicate carvings would take away the breath of any visitor to Bednur. The palace had been lovingly built by her husband, Basappa Nayaka, for his wife. Now, she wouldn't be living here anymore.

All the love that my husband showered on me, all the sweet nothings that I said to him... Our strolls through the courtyard... The best moments of my life were with him in this palace. This palace was the only thing that brought back those cherished memories after he passed away. And now, it will be defiled by Hyder Ali. I can't let this sacrilege happen! I will not let him defile the temple of love my husband built.

With tears in her eyes, she commanded one of her slave girls in a firm voice, 'Hyder Ali does not deserve this palace. Even if he captures Bednur, he should still live in his tent. Burn the palace to the ground.'

As a symbolic gesture, she took a torch and burnt a canopy of the palace. Soon, other maids and soldiers set fire to the wooden palace with all its treasures and gold inside. Leaving behind a flaming palace, Rani Viramma escaped to the nearby fort of Kavaladurga.

While the young soldiers of the Mysore army, invigorated by the hope of the wealth that would soon be theirs, slashed and burnt everything in their way as they moved to the centre of the fort, the veterans of the Mysore army released all their frustration and anger at this year-long siege by killing everyone in sight. By the end of the day, the fort was theirs. Citizens were stripped of their valuables, women were violated and many buildings were burned. After the soldiers had their fill, Hyder entered the city. Mohammed Ali gave him an appraisal of the situation. 'My lord, I have the misfortune of being the bearer of unfortunate news. The rani has burnt her palace with the treasures inside and escaped from Bednur.'

Hyder smiled at Mohammed Ali. He saw a naive man in his general.

'Mohammed Ali, gold only melts in fire, it doesn't vanish. Salvage the burnt structure and extract all the gold, silver and precious stones. I don't care about the palace. Tell the soldiers the plunder must stop at dusk. The people of Bednur are now mine. They will be accorded with the same protection as any other citizen of Mysore. If any soldier continues with the plunder, they will be severely punished. Also, I think the actual treasury of the Bednur kingdom must be outside the palace – look for it.'

Hyder then ordered his spies to track down the rani. He was not going to let her go that easily. Kavaladurga was about twenty kilometres from Bednur. The rani had already reinforced the fort, but not to the scale of Bednur. Having already gone through a long siege, Hyder ordered a direct assault on Kavaladurga, and it fell very quickly to the Mysore troops, who were revitalized after the fall of Bednur.

The Rani was brought back in chains to Hyder. He had set up an outdoor court to look into the administrative affairs of Bednur and deal with the prisoners. Rani Viramma was still in her armour. Her helmet had been taken away and her thick black hair fluttered in the air. There was defiance in her walk, and in her eyes. Meanwhile, Hyder had turned from a bloodthirsty warrior to a keen-eyed administrator. He wore a simple silk dress with a yellow cummerbund around his waist. He was devoid of any jewels. A yellow silk turban covered his head. He was standing and listening to his officers when the rani was brought in.

He did not see an adversary in her. He saw her as just another prisoner but recognized her status as a rani. The meeting between the two was quick. He said, 'I offered you the chance to go to Srirangapatna as my royal guest and you refused. You will now go to Srirangapatna as a common prisoner. You will count your last days in my prison. Take her away!'

Hyder turned his back to her. Rani Viramma wasn't even given a chance to reply. The soldiers yanked the chains around her neck and dragged her out.

The riches of Bednur were beyond Hyder's imagination. He now had a huge source of revenue to fuel his ambitions and secure his safety. He ordered a palace and mint to be built in the city. He had his engineers repair the fort and reinforce its defences. Most of the tributary states of Bednur accepted Hyder as their master immediately after the capture of the capital. Hyder's kingdom grew by more than half. He was so pleased with the climate and its strategic location that he began to consider making Bednur the capital of Mysore. But he first needed to manage all the forts that lay towards the coast, which had not yet accepted his suzerainty.

Two big forts guarded the entire coast – Mangalore and Honnavar. But they were no match to the superior firepower and numbers of Mysore. They soon capitulated. With the surrender of Mangalore, Hyder entered the fort late in the evening. He went directly to the rampart that faced the sea. He was a little nervous and excited at the same time.

All the stories that I have heard about the deep blue sea … The traders carrying their wares as their ship glides over the waves, the pirates that roam the sea waiting to attack merchant ships, the vastness of the waters ... So vast that one sees only blue till the horizon.

He had never seen the sea before.

He was rendered speechless by the majestic scene in front of him. It was more magnificent than what he had imagined; the sheer size of the sea overwhelmed him. He stood stupefied as the cool sea breeze kissed his face. The mighty sun was slowly setting and in time would be swallowed by the water. A sense of fear struck his heart.

Only the bravest of the brave will venture out into the sea. The sun is a mere fireball that will sink without a trace. How can a man in the middle of the sea, who sees water all around him, gather the courage to move ahead? Only the fearless can do it.

The Europeans are indeed a different breed. They have conquered the seas. No wonder they are able to create miracles on land. No obstacle is big enough and no ambition unachievable once one controls the seas.

If I want to be as powerful as them, I must conquer the seas as well. Only the man who controls the seas can control the land.

Hyder got down from the rampart and set up camp in Mangalore.

His army easily overwhelmed the defences of the remaining small forts in the region. The entire coast north of Malabar, up to the Maratha strongholds, now belonged to him. He became one of the few rulers who had control of the coasts.

Some weeks later, at one of the bastions of the Mangalore fort with Lutf Ali Beg and staring at the sea, he said, 'The strength of the Europeans lies in their prowess at sea. They control the sea and hence can trade widely and amass a lot of money. It is this trade that allows them access to limitless resources to wage wars. This is one of the key ingredients of their success.'

He paused and looked at his old general. 'We need to get a stake in the sea. We must establish trade ties with the Ottoman Empire and Europe. We will set up a new branch of the military – we need our own navy.' He continued with his instructions. 'Use the docks of Mangalore and build brigs to protect our coasts and build some trade ships to export our spices and precious stones to the Turks and beyond.'

He was lost in thought for some time, after which he said, 'The future of warfare will be determined by the seas and the future of the world will be decided by the masters of the seas. We need to be ready for this change. Speed up our naval activities. Lutf Ali, ensure that we have these two ports ready to hold our ships for trade and battle. Hire as many skilled people as you can to build these vessels. I'll route some of the revenue from Bednur for this activity. We need a sizeable naval presence at the earliest.'

Having passed on his instructions to his men, Hyder returned to Bednur. Tributes from all the neighbouring regions – Shikaripura, Sagara and Kollur – had reached the capital. Almost half of Mysore's wealth now resided in the treasury of Bednur. Hyder was soon engrossed in the administration of the new province. He ordered his subordinates, 'I want a treasury bigger than the one in Srirangapatna to be built here. We need to hold most of our wealth in the new treasury. Also look into the modalities of transferring the administration from Srirangapatna to Bednur.'

Almost a year after the fall of Bednur, one winter day, Hyder was enjoying a simple meal of rice and meat curry for dinner. When he was done eating, he decided to spend the rest of the evening watching the dancing girls. But then he started to feel the onset of a severe stomach ache. He was immediately taken to his quarters and attended to by his personal physicians. After a few nerve-racking hours of medication and vomiting, the physicians declared that Hyder was out of harm's way. Everyone left his tent except for the chief physician.

Hyder was still weak but his mind was agile. 'All right, Hakeem, tell me what happened.'

'You had been poisoned, my lord. By the grace of God, all the poison has been expelled from your body. You are safe now.'

'Was it in the food?'

'Yes, my lord. This was a powerful poison that acts on ingestion. Your last meal was the root cause.'

'Thank you. You may leave now.'

The hakeem went out of the tent, leaving Hyder alone. In his solitude, he started thinking.

I have faced danger every day back in Srirangapatna but I knew how to survive. I knew all the tricks to keep myself one step ahead. But I haven't had such a close brush with death as I have had here in Bednur. The pleasant climate and the abundant riches hide something more nefarious. I don't think I will be safe here. Srirangapatna may be dry and dusty and a constant target for my enemies. But it is my home and I feel safe there. I need to stay put at home than in this place which masks danger under its beauty.

He had made up his mind to make Bednur his capital, but this assassination attempt made him reconsider his decision. Now he changed his mind. He would move back to Srirangapatna. Bednur was merely another source of wealth, not his home.

After a few days, Hyder recovered enough to hold court again. His spies had identified more than 300 people who were part of the conspiracy to kill him. Hyder was in no mood for mercy and gave orders to execute all of them. He then had two of his loyalists – Venkatachala Rao and Venkatappa, who had been with him from his Dindigul days – installed as diwan and dalwai of Bednur, respectively.

It was time for him to make his move.

9

The end of winter in 1765, Savanur

'BEFORE WE GO HOME, THE NAWAB OF SAVANUR MUST BE punished for his transgressions.'

Hyder had decided to avenge the nawab for attacking his soldiers during the siege of Bednur. Marching to Savanur meant crossing the Tungabhadra River, the traditional southern boundary of the Maratha empire. Even though the Nawab of Savanur had pledged allegiance to the nizam, he was also duty-bound to pay chauth to the Marathas, who saw him as a feudatory. An attack on Savanur was sure to attract the attention of the Marathas. But Hyder was in no mood to let the Nawab of Savanur off the hook.

Hyder's army descended from the lush green ghats of Bednur and entered the arid lands near the Tungabhadra. The river was relatively dry even before the start of summer and the army was able to cross without much difficulty. He was now in familiar territory and challenging familiar enemies.

He camped close to Savanur without initiating a blockade or siege. The plan was to set up camp and rest as the march would be long and arduous. He would launch his attack once his troops had recouped. After the camp was erected, foraging parties set out to get fodder for the horses and food for the soldiers and camp followers. Scouts were sent ahead to see if any reinforcements were being provided to defend Savanur. Spies preparing to infiltrate Savanur were being identified. The usual rigour of a campaign was underway.

The Nawab of Savanur, an Afghan Pathan, soon received news of the arrival of Hyder Ali's forces. The Pathans were renowned for the size and skills of their cavalry. Their horses were prized for their pedigree and were highly sought after by the Marathas and Mughals. They were especially effective as light cavalry and very useful in guerrilla tactics. The Pathans were brave men with one fatal flaw – they did not forgive any slight. So, it was not a surprise that the Nawab of Savanur decided to meet Hyder head on even before an attack was initiated against him.

Dinner was being served to the soldiers. Most of them had retired to their tents. The next shift of sentries was getting ready to take over from the guards at various positions of the camp. This was when Mohammed Ali arrived at Hyder's tent to say, 'My lord, the Pathans are gathering all their cavalry in the fort. They are preparing for an attack against us.'

'Are they crazy? We outnumber them and on this flat ground, they have no tactical advantage. What are they up to?'

'The Pathans are a crazy lot. They are haughty and put their honour and thirst for blood ahead of tactics or diplomacy. We shouldn't be surprised by their foolhardy moves.'

'Get the infantry ready. Ensure that their bodies are filled with lead.'

The next morning, the Pathan horses started marching towards Hyder's camp. The ground was flat and dry, with no trees or shrubs. The brown dust that rose behind the horsemen could be seen from miles away. Stealth was not a priority for the Pathans. Soldiers in Hyder's camp were soon ordered into formation. With the cannons in the centre and the infantry and the kuzzaks protecting the flanks, they were ready to face the Afghans.

As soon as they were in range, Mohammed Ali ordered the cannons to be fired. Cannon fire slammed into the Pathan horses, crushing everything in its way. Their formation broke up. But instead of regrouping, they started screaming hysterically and galloping towards Hyder's formation. The distance was too long to maintain a sustained charge and soon, a mishmash of horses moved forward, the stronger ones in the front and the weaker ones lagging behind. More cannon fire crushed all in its path.

As soon as they were in the range of the infantry, Mohammed Ali ordered the muskets to be fired. The few horses that came close to the camp were shot down, and the Pathan horsemen died right under their horses. The second wave of Pathan cavalry who were a little slow in their charge too fell to the muskets. The last wave of the cavalry tried to spread itself out to avoid being shot, but they were soon swamped and butchered by the kuzzaks.

Without breaking a sweat, Hyder's forces had won the day. Back in the camp, he organized a celebratory dinner for Mohammed Ali and his troops. He said, 'Imbeciles! If only their bravery had been tempered with tact, they would have been formidable. I would have preferred to have them as my friends, but they didn't give me an opportunity to extend a hand of friendship. How sad!'

'The hand of friendship will have to wait, my lord. We are expecting another wave of attacks tomorrow.'

'What? Have they gone mad? Do they want to be massacred? They will leave Savanur empty for me if this continues. Get our troops ready. I want this to end tomorrow. We will take the fort after we have decimated them.'

As expected, despite the rout, the remaining Pathan cavalry mounted another attack the next day. Mohammed Ali followed the same tactics again. Cannon shots broke the formation, musket shots wiped out the more eager soldiers and the kuzzaks mopped up the rest. With the Pathan cavalry defeated, the Mysore army marched into the fort of Savanur. The remaining few infantry officers in the fort were shaken into submission by the cannonade at the fort gates. The victorious general entered the fort and took the remaining soldiers captive. Once the fort was secure, Hyder entered with his entourage. He inspected the palaces, treasury and other important buildings. But he was specifically interested in seeing the stables.

When he arrived at the stables, Hyder said, 'These Pathan horses are the finest in the land. They are an extremely useful addition to our army. Seize all of them and try to cross-breed them with our horses. The Pathans may be foolish, but there is no denying that they have well-bred horses.'

It was time for another feast, this time in Savanur. The celebrations went on through the night. The triumphant Mohammed Ali came over to Hyder, who was intoxicated. 'There is a very small garrison in the Maratha forts of Dharwad and Nargund, and they are just a few days' march from here. If you grant permission, I will capture those forts in your name. Then, the whole plain between the Tungabhadra and Krishna rivers would be yours, my lord.'

Hyder was not in his usual state of mind. The liquor had numbed his thinking capability. In a drunken slur, he said, 'There is only one thing written in my fate: victory. I'm sure the peshwa doesn't mind letting go of two desert towns. Go ahead, extend the boundaries of Mysore further north.'

Mohammed Ali's troops were still high on their spectacular win. He marched towards the provincial capital of the region, Dharwad. The small Maratha garrison was surprised to find the Mysore army this far north. A little warning cannon fire was enough for them to surrender. Placing his soldiers in the fort, he proceeded to Nargund, the other big town in the region.

Even before the troops came to the vicinity of the town, the khiledar of the fort sent emissaries requesting safe passage. He was willing to hand over the keys of the fort in return for the safety of the garrison. Mohammed Ali agreed and let the Marathas leave the fort unharmed. So, with almost minimal losses, a major chunk of the Tungabhadra-

Krishna plain was now controlled by Hyder Ali. Never had Mysore's boundaries been extended this far.

Peshwa Madhav Rao was shocked to hear about Hyder's deep encroachments into Maratha territory. It was always the Marathas who conquered others' lands. He did not expect an upstart like Hyder to have the gall to annex his territories. He quickly left Poona with a staggering army to teach Hyder Ali a lesson. Hyder was still in the vicinity of Dharwad when he received news of the peshwa's movements.

'My spies tell me that the peshwa is bringing an army ten times the size of ours to attack us. What do you propose we do?' he asked his generals.

Lutf Ali Beg said, 'We should retreat. These drylands offer us no tactical advantage. Our guerrilla techniques would not work here.'

Mohammed Ali added, 'We can set up a strong garrison in the conquered forts and make a strategic retreat towards Bednur.'

Hyder thought about the options being presented to him. He knew he had no chance against the Marathas, who were hell-bent on punishing him. 'Let's fall back,' he concurred. 'It would be better if we don't confront the Marathas. Safer to get into wooded terrain, where we have a better chance of defending ourselves. Mohammed Ali, strengthen the garrisons in the captured forts and return soon. Lutf Ali, you lead the retreat towards Bednur. We will set up defensive positions once we are there.'

The Mysore army quickly turned around and started moving towards Bednur. Supplies of lesser value and slow-moving carts and wagons were directed towards Srirangapatna as the rest was being moved into the thick Bednur forests. They hoped that the Marathas would be lured to attack the easy target of supply wagons while leaving the others alone. But Peshwa Madhav Rao was not taken by this bait. He had come to punish Hyder, and he directed his entire force into the forest.

The mainstay of both the armies was their swift cavalry. Hyder tried his best to move back quickly but the large army of the Marathas was catching up with them. He would not make it to Bednur, and would have to give battle somewhere else. The place he chose was Rattihalli. There was just about enough space in this village to put his army into position for battle. But stopping and turning around to get into formation meant the Marathas would catch up with them. This did not give the Mysore army time to set up camp, who had to be hastily put into formation. The cannons were not ready, nor were the infantry prepared for the Maratha attack. Hyder decided that the best way to arrest the movement of the Maratha cavalry was to bring in his kuzzaks against them.

The kuzzaks were sent to challenge the vast Maratha cavalry. The best strategy was to flank them, but the Maratha army was so vast that there was no time to move to a flanking position. Attacking the middle was suicidal.

So, Hyder ordered them to take on only one side of the Maratha army flank.

The kuzzaks moved rapidly to one end of the Maratha cavalry and attacked with such vigour that the enemy's formation was broken. But they could not sustain this for long. Very soon, the entire Maratha cavalry engulfed the kuzzaks. Quite a few of the horsemen were slain. Seeing the death toll rise, Hyder quickly ordered a retreat to cut their losses. During this skirmish of the cavalries, Hyder thought it was prudent to move his slow-moving troops deeper into the woods. With the withdrawal of the kuzzaks, the entire Mysore army had retreated from the field. Hyder had limited his losses to some kuzzaks but had barely saved his own skin.

Luck seemed to favour Hyder as the monsoon arrived and the campaign season came to a pause. It had been four months since the Marathas had marched against Hyder to eliminate the Mysore nawab. Now, both Hyder Ali and Peshwa Madhav Rao were stuck in their positions east of Bednur and were waiting for the monsoon to subside before continuing the war. Hyder's army was holed up in Shikaripura. The slush and the torrential rain made it impossible to move in any direction. The Marathas were very close and would attack the minute the rains subsided. So, Hyder decided to set up a defensive position in Shikaripura.

'The entire Maratha army can't move in a huge formation here. We will set up an ambush right here in this region with our cannons all around. The cannons will be on the high ground surrounding this place – there will be no way out. We will have the kuzzaks draw them into this place. We will force them into the line of musket fire from the infantry. Once they are in, we will let the cannons loose on them. No one will make it out alive.'

The trap was set. Once the rains subsided, the Marathas entered deeper into the thick forests in search of Hyder's forces. The kuzzaks attacked them on this tough terrain and the Maratha cavalry gave them chase. It was a slow and gruelling battle on difficult terrain. As the cavalry cut through the vegetation, they were suddenly accosted with intense musket fire from all sides. The Mysore infantry let loose a barrage of lead on the Marathas. There were losses, but they were insignificant, considering the size of the Maratha army. The experienced cavalry took the losses in their stride and moved ahead in the direction of the least musket fire to slaughter the lightly armoured infantry. The plan was working perfectly. The Maratha cavalry was being drawn into the ambush.

Soon, the entire Maratha army was in the shallow region, right where the Nawab of Mysore wanted them to be. Hyder gave the order to fire the cannons. To his surprise, none of the cannons fired. He was livid. The opportunity was slipping from his hands. 'What's happening? Why aren't the cannons firing?'

'The fuses won't light! They have gone damp!'

By now, the Marathas had figured out that they were in a trap. They saw the cannons pointed towards them. Shouting and howling, they ran towards the impaired cannons. On seeing the fearsome cavalry coming towards them, most of the Mysore soldiers manning the cannons retreated in fear. The ambush had failed. The kuzzaks were already tired, and seeing the Maratha cavalry still active, they too gave up and retreated. The overall retreat of the cavalry and the failure of cannons broke the infantry. The musket fire stopped and everyone ran for their lives. Hyder was left all alone with his personal guards.

A Maratha horseman identified Hyder's standard. 'There he is! Chase him!'

A horde of Maratha horsemen raced towards him. Fearing for his life, his guards quickly took him away. But the Maratha cavalry wouldn't give up and continued chasing them. Cutting through the thick vegetation, Hyder saw his military drummers retreating in the same direction. The drummers were the part of his troops used to maintain discipline. This was one of the things that he had introduced to his forces when he started modelling his army on the Europeans. Hyder cried, 'Stop! Stop!'

The drummers were startled to see the nawab. They bowed down to their master.

'Give me one of your drums. And beat the drums along with me.'

A drummer obliged, and Hyder picked up his drum and started playing it vigorously. 'Come on! Join me. Let's play the marching tune.'

The group started beating the drums in a frenzy. The sound reverberated throughout the forest, making the Maratha cavalry stop in their tracks. One of the soldiers asked, 'What is that sound? Are those military drums?'

'Yes! Has the nawab got reinforcements?'

Fear crept into their hearts. 'We are alone in this unknown terrain, far away from our army. It is not wise to pursue him any further. I propose we turn back.'

The other members of the cavalry agreed. 'We will inform the peshwa about the reinforcements.' And thus, the Maratha cavalry retreated towards the main army.

Meanwhile, Hyder's army had regrouped. He wanted to count his losses, but he first needed to get to safety. He had only just dodged death, but he was still not out of danger. He ordered a march towards Bednur.

After a few days, the exhausted troops entered Bednur. The strong army of Mysore had turned into a bunch of ragged men. Hyder had suffered immense losses, with quite a big chunk of his army deserting him or killed by the Marathas. The only silver lining was that Mohammed Ali's kuzzaks were able to steal some of the horses and cattle from their enemy which had broken away from the main army.

The deafeat had taken its toll on Hyder. His health deteriorated. He was coughing a lot and running a temperature. Soon, he was bedridden. The chief physician attended to him. He said, 'My lord, you need to rest until you get better.'

'I am in the middle of a campaign, Hakeem. How do you expect me to rest?'

'I would recommend you to not continue your campaign. Your poor health is a bigger danger to you than the Marathas. Please listen to me. You need to go home, or else you will not survive.'

'Thank you, Hakeem,' said Hyder and dismissed him. The chief physician rose and left Hyder to himself.

Hyder knew he stood no chance against the Marathas. So he decided to opt for diplomacy.

He sent two emissaries to the peshwa's camp. It turned out that the peshwa too was suffering from poor health. He had suffered losses to his cavalry, and even his supplies were running low, especially after the looting by the kuzzaks. It was in his interest as well to end the campaign. But being the superior force, he wanted the final settlement to be in his favour. After all, he had Hyder pinned down. With this in the back of his mind, he welcomed the emissaries and made his demands.

The emissaries put forth the peshwa's demands to Hyder who listened to them from his bed.

'A demand of thirty-two lakhs as chauth, the surrender of Dharwad and Nargund, the return of Savanur to the nawab and the release of Morari Rao of Gooty, who you captured during your last campaign against them. If we acquiesce, the peshwa will return to Poona.'

Hyder said, 'I can't hold on to Dharwad and Nargund and I have already got the Pathan horses from Savanur. I would have preferred the Pathan nawab's friendship and a steady supply of his horses than rule over Savanur. I have no qualms about giving it up. There is enough money in the Bednur treasury to pay the peshwa. I am only concerned about releasing Morari Rao. I have seen him in action in Gooty when we captured that city. He is a dangerous man who might try to seek revenge.'

He didn't want to think for too long. 'Go back to the peshwa and inform him that I am willing to fulfil all his demands. He should hold his end of the agreement and leave this region. Since he didn't ask me to relinquish Sira, it is now safe to say that Sira is part of Mysore. I will take that as a silver lining in an otherwise grim situation.'

The conquered territories were reverted to their previous owners, the chauth was paid and Morari Rao was freed. Peshwa Madhav Rao held up his end of the deal. He went back to Poona to focus on his health.

With the Marathas out of the way, Hyder returned to Srirangapatna. He was feeling much better, and his ambitions were reignited.

We need to stay away from the Marathas for some time. We must look in another direction to expand. We need resources to sustain our kingdom against our larger neighbours who seem hell-bent on vanquishing us.

10

The monsoon of 1766, Srirangapatna

IT WAS A RARE PERIOD OF CALM IN THE KINGDOM OF MYSORE. The nawab was back in Srirangapatna, and the empire was running smoothly. His mind wasn't on military campaigns but he continued to focus on strengthening his army.

Impressed with the drums that had ssaved his life in the forests of Bednur, he ordered all the Islamic instruments used in the military to be replaced by European percussion instruments.

In a first for his army, he introduced drills for his cavalry. All the drills were to be conducted using the new European tools. Though he had been importing European artillery and battle tactics for some time now, his army didn't have the character of a European army, even if it looked like one. He realized that discipline was one of the secrets of the Europeans' success on the battlefield. It was the difference between a rout and a victory. If he were to defeat the larger armies of the Marathas and the nizam, his troops would have to be disciplined. Drills were essential to inculcate discipline in an army, so they became a part of his army routine.

Until now, he had been hiring French artificers to maintain and handle the cannons. These were French mercenaries who often were merely guns for hire. He now actively sought soldiers from the French East India Company to augment his troops. A French soldier was more effective while assaulting a fort and holding defences during a siege. He raised companies of French soldiers under his pay and even went so far as to offer them a different pay structure, the money exceeding what his highest-paid cavalries made. He reorganized the pay of his own soldiers as well. It was announced that he would pay them for eleven months every year, and the money for the remaining one month would be doled out from the loot of his campaigns. This is how he ensured that his soldiers were always raring to go on campaigns.

French engineers, who were sent across the kingdom to repair and renovate forts, were also hired. A churn of activity resulted in mud forts and ancient forts being replaced by modern, French-designed and French-engineered forts that could withstand intense cannon fire and be formidable symbols of power and authority. The old forts may have lost their originality but they were much more effective now.

Mercenaries were also invited from different parts of the country. Hyder hired Rajputs and their camel guns. He introduced new units of men with matchlocks who would now march with the infantry. They would be in the line of fire before he deployed the muskets. All of the soldiers were given uniforms, which gave them a sense of belonging and made them identify as a part of the Mysore army.

The army itself was divided into two classes for both the cavalry and the infantry; the superior ranks were assigned better equipment and armour. With the increase in the size of the army, different kinds of troops and differentiated classes, the formations on the field were also given a European reboot. His infantry was trained to form infantry squares to face cavalry attacks in the battle. They were trained to march in column formation for more rapid movement while not losing the fighting edge. Hyder positioned his lightly armoured troops to protect the better armoured but heavier and slower troops from the outside during movement and in battle. The transformation of Hyder Ali's army was in full swing.

On the field outside the walls of Srirangapatna Fort, Hyder Ali was watching his troops in action when Lutf Ali Beg approached him and said, 'My lord, I would like you to meet one of our military engineers. He has something very interesting for you.'

A young man in white military fatigues came forward. He had an iron can tied to one end of a thick bamboo stick in his hand. Addressing the nawab, he said, 'With your permission, I would like to give you a demonstration of my invention, my lord.'

Hyder nodded. The engineer took the contraption some distance away from the group. He stuck the bamboo stick into the ground with the iron can on top and brought out a small torch. He lit the small fuse at the end of the can and ran away from the stick. The fuse burned till the end of the can, and all of a sudden, fire blazed out of it, accompanied by a lot of noise and sparks. The entire contraption shot up into the sky and kept going higher, burning all the way and eventually falling almost 500 metres from the launch site.

Hyder was amazed. 'What is this?' he asked in awe.

'It's a rocket, my lord. I filled the iron can with gunpowder, compressed it and tied the can to a bamboo stick. When lit, it shoots up, reaching great heights and covering a large distance.'

Hyder's eyes sparkled. 'The potential of this invention is limitless. This can give us a decisive edge on the battlefield.'

Lutf Ali Beg said, 'I have asked him if he can add a sword to the contraption. Imagine flying swords raining down from the sky, slashing our enemies!'

'Swords? Yes, we can have flaming swords! Imagine burning swords raining down. We will create havoc in the enemy's army! Fund the engineer and give him whatever he needs. Focus on attaching swords and try to increase the range and precision of the rocket. Lutf Ali, I want to see a great outcome from these rockets.'

That day, after finishing up with the army, Hyder returned to his palace to hold court and meet visitors to Srirangapatna. His meetings went on as usual until the last one with Ali Raja. He was the chieftain of the principality of

Kannur, which was a feudatory of the Zamorin of Calicut, the hereditary king of the region. It was a surprise for Hyder to see the chieftain in his court.

'I have come seeking your assistance, my lord. The zamorin has lost interest in his lands. As his vassal, I face nothing but harassment, and I seek freedom from his cruelty. I request you to march into Malabar and relieve us from his tyranny. My Moplah brothers will welcome you and support you when you come into Malabar.'

During his days as the commandant of Dindigul, Hyder had encroached into the Malabar territory. The zamorin had sought peace by promising to pay him. The money had never come through despite the withdrawal of troops, and thus he had a score to settle with the zamorin. At the same time, he wanted to test out his new army and expand the borders of his kingdom. Malabar was far away from all the other major players like the Marathas and the nizam, and there was no danger of confronting them during a campaign.

'I will help you, Ali Raja,' Hyder said. 'Prepare your men to support me when I enter Malabar.'

Two months later, Hyder's new army entered the lush green Malabar from the north. Just like Bednur, there were no roads here, the hills were steep and treacherous with fast-flowing rivers criss-crossing the landscape. It was especially difficult to move his cannons and cavalry. The movement of the infantry was relatively easier, but it was still quite a task for the soldiers. They often had to break formation and move in narrow lines to cover ground faster.

Despite the scenic locale, abundant food and water, there was something peculiar about the region. It was almost as if something was lurking behind the leafy trees, watching them, and it unnerved the soldiers.

The men with the matchlocks were marching ahead of the cannons but behind the scouting cavalry. Sometime during their journey, they found themselves separated from the rest. But they continued to follow the narrow trail made by the cavalry. Out of nowhere, hundreds of half-naked men with crude swords attacked them from all directions. They mercilessly separated heads from bodies. At close quarters, the matchlocks could not be filled with gunpowder and fired. It was a one-sided contest where the attackers were the only ones with weapons. Despite the frantic attack, some of the Mysore men were able to light their matchlocks and fire a few shots but it was not enough – the carnage could not be stopped. Hearing the shots, the cavalry in the rear rushed to the spot. By then, the attackers had vanished into the forest, leaving no trace.

The local guide to the army informed the cavalry commander, 'Those were the Nairs, loyal to the zamorin. They can't face us in a fair fight, and so they resort to these tactics. They know the terrain well and can come and go with ease. We must reach Calicut quickly before we are attacked like this again.'

The cavalry commander ordered his men, 'Keep the cavalry with the infantry. Ensure that the matchlocks and muskets are always loaded. We must be ready to meet their blades at any instant.'

The army regrouped for greater safety but it slowed down the movement of the troops. It would take them longer to reach the zamorin's capital, and they would face further attacks from the Nairs. The easiest targets were the lightly armoured infantry, the matchlocks. Everyone else was either heavily guarded or heavily armoured. The Nairs did not stop their attacks. Every day they would attack when the group split up or when they were in a vulnerable position. It was almost as if they were watching the Mysore army constantly and attacking at the most opportune time. Hyder's men were not able to track them – they simply vanished into thin air after each attack. The army's losses were mounting higher but Hyder forced them to move ahead.

The army finally arrived at the mouth of a river connected to a larger river. The Nairs had made a stand there. This would be a direct fight. Hyder ordered his musketeers into formation. The Nairs were no match for his army but they had greater numbers. The musketry moved into range; Hyder ordered them to fire. It was a massacre. Rather than retreating to safety, the Nairs ran straight towards the gunshots, but most of them fell. The ones who survived were mowed down by the cavalry. Thus the last stand of the Nairs was ruthlessly put down.

As the Mysore army got closer to Calicut, the Moplah peasants joined them. They were more useful as guides than as an armed force. They quickly guided the army through the wooded forests to Calicut with minimal losses. Calicut did not have a proper fort, and it would be easy pickings for the Mysore army. The zamorin was aware of this. He immediately came to Hyder's camp, asking for peace. The frail, old zamorin, in a submissive posture, would have evoked sympathy in any man with a heart. The large-hearted Hyder Ali was no exception.

Hyder respectfully bowed in front of the old man. He then stood upright in front of him and addressed the zamorin in a firm but steady tone, 'I know you have come to pledge your allegiance to me.'

'Yes, my lord. I will pledge my allegiance to you – I only ask for peace.'

'I also want peace. This campaign has been long and hard for me. I ask for only one thing – compensate for my military expenditures, and I will go back.'

'Of course. I will make the necessary payments. With your permission, I will go back to my palace, speak with my accountants and arrange the money.'

'Why take the hassle of going back to the palace? Send your ministers, please stay as my guest. There is a big temple nearby, and you can stay there with your entourage.'

The zamorin looked helpless. He had come to meet Hyder without any soldiers, and he was surrounded by the Mysore army. He had no choice but to accept the proposal.

Later that evening, Hyder was alone with Lutf Ali Beg. He said, 'The zamorin did not pay me last time, and I don't trust him to pay this time either. We will keep him in the temple until he gives us the money that is due to us. Then, we end this horrendous campaign.'

'With your permission, I will cut off Calicut from the rest of the region. We shouldn't have any more surprises from the forests.'

'Yes, go ahead. Use every method you know to get the money from his ministers. I don't want to stay here too long.'

As expected, the zamorin's ministers were not able to arrange the money. They tried to buy time and have the zamorin released, but Hyder refused to let him go. Slowly, cajoling turned to coercion, and physical threats soon followed. But no money came forth.

Lutf Ali Beg ordered his soldiers, 'Confine the zamorin alone and post guards outside. He must feel the pressure.'

To make matters worse, the soldiers of Mysore physically abused the Zamorin's retainers in front of the Zamorin before taking them away. The old king was reduced to tears. That night, after dinner, he couldn't stop weeping over his helpless situation.

People who have trusted me are now suffering because of me and I can't do anything to end their misery. I am helpless. I can't take the humiliation any longer.

Steeling himself, the zamorin wiped his tears as he looked around. He was alone inside the inner chamber of the temple. He saw a torch fixed on the wall and picked it up.

If I can't help my people in their hour of need, I don't deserve to be their king. I have failed in my duty to protect them. I don't deserve to live.

Gripping the torch in his trembling hands, the zamorin set everything combustible in his room on fire. He moved to the adjacent rooms and did the same thing. The fire immediately engulfed the door, windows, curtains, everything. He sat in the middle of his room, his face expressionless, as the fire swallowed him up as well.

The soldiers stationed outside were late to react. They used mud and water to stop the growing fire but to no avail. Hyder himself rushed to the temple and helped the soldiers extinguish the fire but it was all in vain. The flames had completely burnt the temple down, along with the zamorin.

Hyder was aghast when he heard about the death of the zamorin in the fire.

The poor man! He put his honour ahead of his life. I shouldn't have pushed him so much. I needlessly got him killed. Now, he is no more.

He said to Lutf Ali Beg, 'Cremate the zamorin with full state honours. The people of Malabar are now the citizens of Mysore. They will be accorded the same protection as every other subject in our kingdom.'

With the death of the zamorin, the rulers of Palakkad and Cochin, who were vassals of the zamorin, surrendered to Mysore's might. All of Malabar was now under Hyder Ali's control.

11

The end of winter in 1766, Calicut

AS THE CITY OF CALICUT FELL INTO MOURNING AFTER THE death of its beloved zamorin, Hyder Ali's officers checked the treasury and found that there was not enough money to meet their nawab's demand. The zamorin had indeed been helpless and was never in a position to pay Hyder. The Mysore accountants took whatever valuables they could find and added them to Hyder's accounts.

With not much to gain, Lutf Ali Beg recommended going home. 'We need to return before the start of the monsoon. Otherwise, we will be stuck here with no way out.'

'Yes, there is no point staying here. Order the troops to move to Dindigul. We will deal with some of the rebellious palegars before going home,' declared Hyder.

After appointing a governor for the Malabar region, he marched towards Dindigul. Along the way, he extracted tribute from local chieftains and punished those who stood up to him.

A messenger arrived from Srirangapatna while Hyder was in the middle of his drive against the local palegars. One of his writers read out the letter: 'Krishnaraja Wodeyar passed away in Srirangapatna. You are requested to name the next king of Mysore.'

Hyder was silent for some time, taking in this sudden piece of news. Then he quickly collected himself. 'This is not a good time for me to go home. Write a letter to the diwan asking him to crown Nanjaraja Wodeyar, Krishnaraja's eldest son, as the new king. It is not appropriate or prudent to keep the throne empty. I will finish this campaign and go meet with the new king.'

The message was sent over to Srirangapatna and Nanjaraja Wodeyar was crowned the king of Mysore. After his campaign in Dindigul, Hyder marched back to home.

It had been a long time since he had seen his family. After Fatima and Tipu were sent to Gurramkonda, Hyder had barely had a chance to meet them. But now, with Tipu's education complete, his family was back in the capital.

As Hyder walked to his palace, he saw his sixteen-year-old son Tipu eagerly waiting for him in the courtyard. Fatima was in the ladies' quarters. On seeing Tipu, now as tall as his father and dressed in the finest silks, the richest jewellery and the most elaborately designed headgear, Hyder felt proud.

Tipu appears like a prince! He looks more like the son of a sultan than a general. I have done a good job of raising him. I have given him all the things I never got in my life. Now look at him! A veritable prince!

Tipu bowed respectfully. 'Hello, father. It is good to have you back home.'

Hyder hugged him, 'Tipu, my boy, it's good to see you. You have grown to be a well-groomed man. I hope you have learned all the arts and developed your skills at Gurramkonda.'

'Yes, father. I have been trained by the best teachers. You had hired the very best. I am now putting my education to good use. I am assisting Lutf Ali Sahib in the administration of the kingdom and I am actively taking part in the military drills with Mohammed Ali Sahib.'

Grabbing Tipu by his shoulders, Hyder took a good look at his son. He beamed with pride and held his son.

The light of my life.

'It's good to hear that, son. I will now visit your mother.'

Releasing Tipu, he moved on to the ladies' quarters.

On seeing Hyder enter the quarters, Fatima instructed her maids to leave the chamber, leaving the two alone. She rushed towards her husband, hugging him tightly. Hyder returned the embrace with equal intensity.

He slowly separated himself from his wife to look at her face. Tears were rolling down her cheeks. Fatima's voice choked as she said, 'I missed you.'

Hyder smiled at her and hugged her again, caressing her head which he held close to his chest. He blinked away the tears that were threatening to spill from his eyes.

After spending time with his family, he moved to his court late in the evening. The first task on his agenda was to hear the contents of the letters addressed to him. The first one stunned him. 'The king of Mysore, Nanjaraja Wodeyar, has hereby declared that the dalwai can carry out war operations and troop movements only with the king's permission.'

The newly crowned king's first order was to put his commander under his control. He had clearly not gauged the true power of his dalwai.

A shocked Hyder shouted, 'What? Has he lost his mind? Does he realize the consequences of proclaiming this nonsense? Summon Mohammed Ali at once.'

As soon as Mohammed Ali arrived, Hyder said, 'Go to the king's palace. Confiscate all the treasures and stores, move the royal family from the palace to a smaller home meant for one of our junior ministers. That should teach him a lesson.'

Mohammed Ali marched into the king's palace and did as Hyder had ordered. The king had always been a puppet but at least he led the life of a king with all its riches and benefits. But now, the king was stripped of any semblance of grandeur; he was a mere prisoner.

The news of Nanjaraja Wodeyar's situation reached Poona and agitated Peshwa Madhav Rao. Hyder was growing stronger with every passing year. Imprisoning the king would only strengthen his hold over Mysore, and worse, legitimize his rule over Mysore. The peshwa would need to intervene, and so he decided to march to Mysore with his troops once again.

A few weeks later, spies arrived at Hyder's court in the night with urgent messages. 'The Nairs have revolted, my lord. The governor and the commandant at Calicut have been murdered. With the monsoon having begun, the rivers are in full spate and our garrison is trapped in Calicut.'

'How did this happen?'

'The governor got greedy and levied taxes in excess to what you had prescribed. The commandant needlessly killed people. Their actions were the trigger for this revolt.'

Taking his army to Malabar was a time-consuming exercise and it was next to impossible to enter and move around in the rains, let alone fight the Nairs. Hyder was still with his spies when his retainer informed him that Mohammed Ali wanted to speak with him urgently. The spies were dismissed and Mohammed Ali came in.

He said, 'The Marathas have attacked us again. Morari Rao of Gooty has already moved south while Peshwa Madhav Rao is crossing the Tungabhadra as we speak. It's possible that they are coming for the chauth.'

Hyder was visibly frustrated.

My whole life has been about escaping the wrath of the Marathas. When will I be free from their tyranny?

Addressing his general, Hyder said, 'Why are they so adamant about the chauth? I have too many problems to deal with right now, but the Marathas will always be the first. Send our ambassadors to them as soon as possible. I want to buy out their military campaign.'

Two ambassadors were immediately sent to the peshwa's camp, with the authority to placate the peshwa by any means possible. War was to be avoided at all costs. The ambassadors came back with the peshwa's demand of thirty-four lakh rupees. Hyder didn't have enough money in his treasury, so he offered seventeen lakhs immediately and pledged the future revenue of the districts near the Tungabhadra for the remaining amount. The ambassadors were successful in their negotiations, and the peshwa returned to Poona. But, Morari Rao continued to plunder the border towns of Mysore. Hyder didn't have the time to address these transgressions. He had to move to Malabar to quell the revolt.

Within a month after negotiating peace with the Marathas, the army marched in incessant rain and across slushy terrain, stopping nowhere. It was difficult but Hyder was hell-bent on crushing the rebellion. Most of the trails made during the previous campaign had been washed away. But using cartographers who had mapped the region during his previous expedition, the army forged ahead towards Calicut. A young and ambitious Nair, Kumaran Nambiar, offered to help Hyder. He showed them a safe path to Calicut and provided supplies to the Mysore army. Thanks to his help, they were able to move quickly, cross rapids, dense forests and slushy grounds in their way and avoid facing any guerrilla attacks by the rebel Nairs.

The bad weather had forced most of the Nairs to remain in Calicut to resist Hyder's army. Hyder Ali's retribution was swift and brutal. The city was quickly reclaimed from the rebels. He spent the next few days undoing the wrongs done by his now-dead governor and commandant. He reduced the taxes and offered amnesty to several nobles of the region to win over their loyalty.

Sitting in the courtyard of his makeshift palace in Calicut, he was listening to his writers who were apprising him of the condition of the region. Even as the writers spoke, Hyder's mind went back to the Nairs who had refused to submit to him and were being lined up to be taken to prison.

These rebels will rise again. No matter what I offer them, they will resist me. I cannot allow another mindless massacre. They are my subjects and I need to take a humane approach. I need to take them to Mysore and make them see the benefits of living under the Mysore administration. They need to be convinced that their lives will be better under me than living in an archaic era here. I need to inspire them to lead better lives. I need to educate them. With good training, they can be loyal subjects of Mysore.

He called on his local commanders, 'The prisoners are good warriors. Offer them freedom if they choose to join my army. I will provide them with the best training. They will be equipped with the best arms and ammunition. They will be given all material benefits and trained in Srirangapatna. If they refuse to take up this offer, the only other option for them is brutal death.'

Fifteen thousand Nairs, who could potentially be a threat to his empire, chose life and were sent to Srirangapatna to be educated and integrated into the empire. Meanwhile, Hyder had more ideas to consolidate his power in the region and to subdue any future rebellion. He ordered a fort to be built in Calicut to house the administration and garrison.

As a reward for the young Kumaran Nambiar who had helped him, Hyder named him the new governor of the region. The Moplahs had also actively helped in his campaign by assisting his cartographers to identify a gap in the mountains connecting Palakkad to Coimbatore, and they were rewarded well for their contributions. Hyder realized that Palakkad offered the easiest way into Malabar. He had to have a strong presence there, so he ordered his French engineers to build a massive fort there as well, which could hold a large garrison and announce the authority of the Mysore kingdom. This fort would be the capital of the region.

Having sorted out all the issues in Malabar, Hyder decided to return to Srirangapatna through Palakkad. On his arrival, he found that most of the Nairs who had been sent to Srirangapatna had not made it to the capital. The unfamiliar climate had had an adverse effect on their health, and most of them perished before they could even reach the capital. His plan of re-education had failed. He realized that the Nairs would not be able to acclimatize to the climate of the region. He needed to deal with Malabar differently.

While discussing his campaign in Malabar with Lutf Ali Beg, he said, 'Malabar will be a problem in the near future. I need quick access to it to quell any possible rebellion.

But with the Marathas in the north, it is difficult to focus on Malabar.'

Lutf Ali Beg offered a solution. 'The kingdom of Coorg connects Mysore with Malabar and offers an easy and quick path to the region. The raja there used to pay tribute to the Rani of Bednur. Technically, you have a right over their lands.'

Hyder seemed eager to know more about Coorg, so Lutf Ali continued, 'Almost all the troublesome palegars around Srirangapatna seek refuge there when our soldiers chase them. So, it is in the best interests of Mysore to absorb Coorg.'

'People of the forest are hardy and brave, but they are also barbaric and difficult to handle. We have seen this in Bednur and Malabar. Are the Coorgis the same?'

'I think they are worse – far braver and more brutal. They follow an animistic religion and are secluded from the other major powers in the region, making them completely different from the rest of the forest people. But my spies tell me that they don't have strength in numbers, and will not be able to withstand an assault from your disciplined army.'

'Well, it's time I paid Coorg a visit.'

'My lord, if I may, your son Tipu has finished his education. He has been training with me and my commanders. It would be good for him to accompany you on this campaign.'

'Of course! He needs to join me one day or the other. This will give him good experience.'

The war veterans of the Malabar campaign were ordered to prepare for the forthcoming visit to the region. Coorg lay south of Bednur and north of Malabar. Its proximity to Srirangapatna surprised Hyder.

I can't fathom how this kingdom had been left alone so far. They could have attacked Srirangapatna anytime just by walking out of the forest. This region has to be absorbed to ensure the safety of Mysore.

The army was now experienced enough to handle the tough terrain of dense forests. Aware of the fact that they might be vulnerable to guerrilla attacks, they had changed their movements to mitigate the damage from those ambushes when they moved into the thick forests of Coorg. The Coorgis were just as brave, if not braver, than the Malabar Nairs but unlike the Nairs, they chose to meet Hyder's forces head on right from the start.

They had gathered near the banks of a stream and were waiting for their adversaries. Unfortunately, their bravery was not accompanied by strategic thinking. They had occupied the lower ground which put them at a disadvantage when attacked from an elevated position. But the war cries and dances of the Coorgi men would have sown the seeds of doubt in any man who thought they were on stronger ground. Hyder's scouts located this army and reported back to the generals. The Mysore army quickly pulled into formation for the assault and climbed up the hills to face the Coorg army.

The Raja of Coorg was stunned in the face of the sheer numbers of the Mysore troops, their uniforms and their guns. He had never seen a disciplined force before. The simple men of Coorg associated victory on the field to individual bravery and valour, but times had changed. A disciplined army with modern tactics could rout any brave army. The Raja of Coorg, however, did not lose heart. He let out a war cry, commanding his men to tear down every man on the other side. His men echoed his war cry with a threatening ferocity. The whole forest reverberated with their voices.

Without waiting for the signal, some Coorgis charged forward. Soon, the rest of the men followed, baying for their enemies' blood. As soon as they were in range, the musketeers from Mysore released a barrage of gunshots, and the entire hill and its surroundings were filled with smoke. The valiant Coorgi men collapsed one after another. But that did not stop them; they kept rushing forward. There was another volley of gunshots. Another round of Coorgi men fell to the gunfire. The remaining choked in the smoke of the gunpowder. Still, they did not yield and pushed on, sprinting tirelessly. The final wave of attacks from the Mysore army was yet to come. The heavily armoured cavalry rushed down like a mighty wave, washing away the remaining Coorgi men. Whoever was still standing after this carnage chose to retreat deep into the forest. It was another absolute victory for Hyder.

Tipu, who was at the rear of his father's army before the fight began, had thought of something unconventional. He said to his commanders, 'I am sure the Coorgis will retreat before the onslaught of my father's men. But they are bound to attack us again in the next few days. What if we cut off their retreat?'

The young commanders reporting to him agreed to his proposal eagerly. They would, after all, be getting a piece of the action. 'Let's get behind their lines and trap them during their retreat. Let's go!'

Without informing Lutf Ali Beg, Tipu rushed away with his troops from the battlefield to occupy strategic positions behind the enemy lines – but they got lost in the forest instead. They slowed down, trying to trace the trail of the enemy. Soon, they found some people hidden amidst the thick leaves and trees. 'I think there is someone ahead. Let's get close and charge at them.'

The other party seemed to be stationary, and there were no signs of retreat. On getting close, Tipu ordered an attack against them.

As they charged ahead, a female voice rang through the air, 'Please don't harm us! Mercy! We are innocents!' It was a camp filled with women and children.

Tipu ordered his cavalry to break the charge. His men quickly surrounded the women and children. Addressing the eldest women who came forward, Tipu asked, 'Who are you?'

'We are the kin of the Raja of Coorg. We have made camp here while our men have gone ahead to fight the Mysore army.'

Tipu was surprised to see womenfolk on the battlefield. He thought it was a strange custom. Nevertheless, this discovery was important. He could now hold them captive and force the Raja of Coorg into submission. He said,

'Arrest them all,' he said. 'Take them to my father's camp. My father will decide what to do with them.'

Back in Hyder's camp that night, the nawab summoned his son to the war council. Tipu came into the tent and bowed to his father.

'Well done, my son. With the raja's wife and children in our hands, they are bound to negotiate with us.'

'Thank you, Father.'

'As a reward for your bravery, you will be allowed to raise 500 horses and 1,000 infantry under your command.'

Tipu bowed again before being dismissed.

As expected, the next morning, ambassadors representing the Raja of Coorg asked for an audience with Hyder. The nawab demanded Coorg's complete submission to Mysore in return for the safety of their women and children. The raja had no option but to accept the suzerainty of Mysore.

With the surrender of the raja, Hyder marched into the capital of Coorg, Madikeri. He held court there for a few weeks. Having learnt from his experience in Malabar, he ordered the construction of a big fort in Madikeri to display Mysore's power and house a garrison of Mysore soldiers.

With the conquest of Coorg, Hyder's empire now stretched from the southern bank of the Tungabhadra in the north to the end of the Malabar forests in the south. He controlled a considerable length of the coast on the west and was competing directly with the nizam for the provinces on the east. Hyder Ali's power had finally come of age.

12

The monsoon of 1767, Srirangapatna

IT WAS THE THIRD LETTER THE NIZAM HAD SENT TO HYDER after the latter had failed to respond to the first two. Hyder was exasperated by what he heard when the letter was read out in his court. 'If the nizam can't hold on to his lands, that is his problem. He still lives under the illusion that I am willing to be his vassal. What do I have to gain by taking on the English?'

While the Marathas, the nizam and Hyder were fighting for the supremacy of all lands south of the Vindhyas, the English under Robert Clive were gnawing at the Mughal territories in the north. Through one battle after another, they had swallowed most of the eastern provinces of the Mughals. They now controlled a territory bigger than the nizam and almost as vast as that of the Marathas. The English had made the transition from a mere trader to a kingdom without raising any alarm amongst its neighbours. But more importantly, they controlled the rich territories of Bengal, Bihar and Orissa which were generating revenues far more than the Maratha or the nizam's territories. Their financial power was far superior to that of the natives and they were now in a position to sustain large-scale warfare.

Though the English assiduously avoided any conflicts with the major powers of the Deccan, the borders of their Bengal empire touched those of the nizam and the Marathas. With the nizam being the weaker of the two, the English began encroaching on his territories both from the north under the Bengal army and the south under the Madras army.

The nizam on his own could not challenge the now-powerful English but he wanted to get back at them. The one man who could still challenge the English was Hyder Ali and the nizam still believed Hyder Ali was his feudatory by virtue of the nizam's status as the successor of the Mughals in the Deccan. He had been writing to Hyder to stem the tide of the English by attacking the latter's smaller southern kingdom around Madras.

In his letters, the nizam had asked Hyder to aid him in attacking the English and recovering the territories annexed by them. But Hyder felt that the nizam was not competent enough to hold on to his lands. Moreover, he did not see himself as a feudatory of the nizam. Nor did he have any intention of getting involved in the nizam's conflicts with the English. In fact, he saw the nizam as a greater threat than the English. He was not inclined to help the nizam at all, but a minister in his court provided a different perspective.

Hyder's minister saw something of value in the nizam's proposition. The Sultan of Mysore could settle some old scores. Putting his proposal across, the minister said, 'Wallajah is an ally of the English. If we attack the English, we would have to annex much of Arcot's territory to reach the English forts. That would be a good exercise – defeating Wallajah.'

Hyder warmed up to the idea the moment Wallajah's name was brought up.

This is a good opportunity to smite the treacherous Wallajah. I will finally be able to do justice for the wrongs that have been done to Shahbaz and Nanjaraja.

'I can't fathom why the English still trust and entertain traitors like Wallajah. If this campaign can give me the opportunity to defeat him, I am willing to mobilize all my troops. Also, I can't antagonize the nizam any further. I'd better humour his demand. The last thing I want is for Salabat Jung to march on Mysore.'

Hyder sent a letter agreeing to the nizam's proposal, expressing his willingness to discuss the modalities. The discussions went on for a while before the agreement between the nizam and Hyder was finalized. After that, Hyder prepared his forces, sorted out the finances and set up the supply lines. Finally, a date for Hyder's forces to join with the nizam's just south of Rayakottai, a fort under Mysore's control, was fixed.

A true soldier and a man of his word, Hyder marched south to the rendezvous point and set up his camp. The undisciplined troops of the nizam could not make it on time and camped on the edge of the nizam's territory.

English spies had not yet got wind of Hyder's movement, and this was a chance that couldn't be wasted. Without waiting for the nizam's forces, Hyder started capturing all the forts and strategic points in Arcot under English control through bribery, sieges and sometimes by storming into the fort. Since the main plan was to go to Madras, the capital of the English in south India, and defeat them, he placed small garrisons in each of the captured forts and went ahead with his main army intact.

Wallajah was alarmed by Hyder's movements and informed they that he was willing to finance their counter-campaign and provide supplies, but he would not be able to put soldiers on the ground. The English were in desperate need of additional troops. But in a situation like this, they didn't mind Wallajah's proposition – any help was acceptable. The English mounted their first defence against Hyder Ali at Kaveripuram.

Through all of this, the nizam didn't move out of his camp. He was waiting for Hyder to do all the work for him. Despite his nonchalant attitude, Hyder continued to hope that the nizam would eventually join the campaign. It was a tough siege at Kaveripuram with Hyder's forces going up against the English infantry.

Meanwhile, the English generals were in a meeting at Fort St George in Madras to decide the course of the battle. The war council called in Colonel Smith.

A young man of medium height with thick blond hair and a face so tanned that he looked like a native, entered the room. He was dressed in a bright red coat and white trousers. Even though he was born in India, he was sweating profusely in the heat of Madras.

On entering the room, he saluted the men who were seated.

The oldest person in the room said, 'Ah, yes! Colonel Smith. Come in, please take a seat.'

Thanking the council member, Colonel Smith sat down.

'As you might be aware, we have opposed the Nawab of Mysore, Hyder Ali, at Kaveripuram. I don't think we can hold him back much longer. We need a plan of action to gain an upper hand in this war.'

Colonel Smith said, 'We need to open another front, sir. I would recommend we seek the assistance of Bombay to create a new front on the western coast. This should force the Nawab of Mysore to devote resources to his western provinces, and thus offer us some relief on this side.'

All the council members nodded in agreement. The oldest member said, 'Very good, Colonel. We will get in touch with our governor in Bombay and seek military assistance.'

Colonel Smith wasn't finished.

'Also, sir, Kaveripuram is a lost cause. We can make a stand at Kanchipuram. But we need to dissuade the nizam from combining his troops with that of the Mysore nawab. I propose we attack the nizam's forces that are beyond the ghats and force him to sue for peace with us. This should isolate the Mysore forces on the east.'

'Thank you, Colonel. I appreciate your sagacious advice. I would seek the consent of the council with regards to this plan.'

The council members needed no convincing. They vigorously nodded in agreement.

The oldest member said, 'Well, it's decided then. Colonel Smith, I would like you to lead our forces against the nizam. Godspeed!'

Colonel Smith rose from his chair, saluted the members and left the room. There was a determined look on his face. A man of focus, he knew the magnitude of the task at hand.

The English troops for the expedition were already primed for battle. Colonel Smith moved swiftly. As the English forces got closer to the nizam's forces, they saw only disorder.

There was no structure or form. The cavalry was away from the main tents and the artillery was abandoned at one end of the camp. It was almost an open invitation to attack. When the English troops reached the grounds held by the nizam, Colonel Smith deployed his infantry towards the artillery. The attack was subdued. The nizam's cannons didn't fire, and the cavalry wasn't aware of the English movement. It was only after the enemy attack was fully underway that the nizam issued orders against the English infantry, but it was too late to make an impact now. The English sepoys dislodged the soldiers operating the artillery with ease and took away all the cannons. The nizam's forces were now without any artillery. Predictably, panic had set in within the nizam's camp.

The loss of their artillery weakened the morale of his men, and they retreated deeper into their territory, fearing another disastrous attack from the English. The general under the nizam started secret negotiations with the English commander, suing for peace and ensuring that the English would not attack them again.

The negotiations were taking place without Hyder's knowledge, who still assumed that the nizam was his ally. Hyder was in his tent discussing the course of the war with his generals. 'The English are a stubborn lot. They just won't give up. How many more cavalry attacks will it take to dislodge them?'

'We need to use our cannons more effectively, picking up strategic points against the English. We can weaken them before unleashing our cavalry.'

The generals continued proposing different ways of attack and alternative tactics to defeat the English when a messenger arrived inside the tent. 'My lord, the English have landed on the western coast and captured Mangalore. They are preparing to attack Bednur.'

Hyder stood up from his masand, stunned. 'What? Mangalore captured! We can't let them capture Bednur at any cost. Raise the siege. We must go to Mangalore now.'

Assigning a few soldiers to this theatre of war, he ordered the bulk of his army to march towards Mangalore. He covered an astonishing 500 kilometres in a matter of days by marching day and night. The small English garrison in Mangalore was stunned to see the forces of Mysore at their gates. Nobody had expected Hyder to move from one end of the peninsula to the other end in such a short duration.

Hyder ordered the cannons to blast the walls of the fort. The English solciers, fearing for their lives, surrendered before the canons were even fired. The new front opened by the English was nipped in the bud. But Hyder was now convinced that this was going to be a long campaign – the English wouldn't give up easily. He soon got busy recruiting more troops and raising money from the Bednur province.

The English on the other end of the peninsula didn't want to let go of the opportunity to reverse their losses. Colonel Smith was in his tent south of the ghats. He had just finished reading the intelligence reports that had come in from Mangalore. He ordered his manservant to bring in his second-in-command, Colonel Wood.

A young man, rather a boy showing the first signs of a beard, entered the tent. He was taller than Colonel Smith but much thinner. He looked more like an apprentice than a colonel. He spoke in a high-pitched voice, 'You called for me, sir?'

'Yes, Wood. Please have a seat. I have some interesting intelligence from Mangalore. It looks like Nawab Hyder Ali has recaptured Mangalore. He will be back soon. We need to make the best use of the time before he arrives.'

'What do you propose, sir?'

'Most of the forts captured by the Mysore troops in the Arcot region are thinly garrisoned. We can easily recapture them and build a buffer against a future assault by the nawab.'

'That's a very good idea, sir. I have been in correspondence with the Nawab of Arcot, Wallajah. He fears for his life. He believes Nawab Hyder Ali is going to come back to kill him. He has offered us additional supplies and money to support our cause against Mysore.'

'What about men?'

'Unfortunately, he is still not willing to commit his men for battle.'

Colonel Smith got to thinking. He wanted to extract the best from the situation at hand. 'Wood, I have a plan. We will gladly accept his help with respect to supplies and money. But ask his men to garrison the forts across Arcot.'

'Yes, sir.'

Wallajah, who was watching from the side lines, saw the prospect of recouping the losses that he had incurred with the incursion of Hyder Ali into his territories. He gladly accepted the English proposal to have his own men garrison all the captured forts. He also offered to provide supplies from these forts to the English soldiers marching towards Mysore territory. With this agreement in place, the English shifted gears to go on an offensive. The English troops proceeded to Bangalore and promptly laid siege to the city.

Colonel Smith and Colonel Wood led the English army on the same path that Hyder took but in reverse and started recapturing all the forts and strategic points. Most of these forts were not heavily guarded, so it was easy to recapture them.

Hyder, who was in Bednur collecting tributes, was startled yet again by the new developments. 'Where are the nizam's forces? Didn't they put up a fight with the English?'

'They are nowhere in the vicinity of Bangalore, my lord. They have withdrawn into their own territory.'

'That coward! I can't lose the second-largest city in my empire. We will march to Bangalore right now!'

The Mysore army once again sped through the ghats and the dry plains to reach Bangalore. Hyder feared the worst but they were in a good place. The commandant at Bangalore Fort had decided to take up the gauntlet thrown by the English and had withstood the siege. Since the English had already occupied the strong ground near the fort, Hyder was forced to occupy the opposite grounds.

Unlike his other adversaries, the English negated the effects of Hyder's cannons with their own precise long-range cannons. They put up stiff resistance to the waves of attack from the kuzzaks, inflicting heavy losses on Mysore's forces. Hyder knew he could not break the English with his usual tactics. He had to try something new.

He told Lutf Ali Beg, 'We can't defeat the English troops like this. Let's go back to disrupting their supply chain instead.'

'Wallajah is sending supplies to the English. It should be an easy task to cut them off.'

'Get inside their territory and choke all the supplies. I will hold the English here.'

With the new orders from his nawab, Lutf Ali Beg went to the plains under Wallajah's control. The kuzzaks played their usual role and cut off all the supplies to the English, who were now pretty much stranded in Bangalore. Meanwhile, Hyder harassed the English troops with his light troops to ensure that they would not make any attempt to storm the fort.

Within a few weeks, the impact of Hyder's plan was evident. Ammunition was depleting in the English camp and there was a steady decline in other supplies as well.

Colonel Smith and Colonel Wood had returned to the camp one evening after fending off yet another attack by the kuzzaks. A couple of servants put up a table and two chairs outside Colonel Smith's tent. The exhausted English officers sat down. Another servant brought steaming tea in a kettle. A couple of ceramic teacups were placed on the table and tea was served.

Colonel Wood was the first to break the silence between the two.

'I don't think it is feasible to hold the siege any longer, sir. We will lose all our soldiers very quickly in this battle of attrition.'

Colonel Smith, who was sipping tea, placed his cup back on the table and said, 'We are stuck between a rock and a hard place, Wood. Do you think the nawab will leave us alone if we retreat? He will hunt us down. We have to fight him either way. I would prefer holding ground on his territory than have him chase us over the ghats.'

Colonel Wood remained silent.

At that moment, a messenger arrived at the English camp with a letter for Colonel Smith.

Opening the leather pouch, Colonel Smith pulled the letter out. As he perused it, a smile broke on his face.

'The nizam has reached an agreement with the English diplomats. I need to go and finalize the agreement with him.'

Colonel Smith paused for a moment. He gathered his thoughts on what to do next.

'We have to lift the siege now, Wood. I will head east with my troops tomorrow morning. You leave the heavy artillery behind and break camp by evening. You don't have much supplies to carry anyway. Make haste towards Madras. Leave behind anything that will slow you down.'

Colonel Wood merely smiled at the sudden change in Colonel Smith's opinion about the siege.

'Yes, sir.' He was relieved.

At least the siege will be lifted. We were surely going to get killed if we stayed here any longer.

The next morning, Colonel Wood broke camp immediately after Colonel Smith left with his troops. All the artillery and its ammunition were left behind. Anything heavy and of low value were also abandoned. Raising the siege, Colonel Wood ordered his troops to head south to safer grounds close to Madras.

When Hyder received intelligence about Colonel Smith's movement to the nizam's territory, he assembled his generals to deliberate on his next move. 'Colonel Smith is going towards the nizam's camp. The nizam has not moved from his last camp. He didn't even bother to back me here. I don't think he is on our side.'

Lutf Ali Beg added, 'The nizam's troops did not help us even once in this entire campaign. You are right, my lord, he is not on our side. Betrayal is in their blood. I just hope they don't turn against us.'

'The nizam is not a priority right now, Lutf Ali. We need to face the English before they regroup. Colonel Wood is on his way back to Madras with a smaller contingent. We should intercept him and pay him back for entering our territory.'

'Yes, my lord. I'll ready the troops. The engineer who was working on the rockets is in Bangalore now. We can get some rockets from him and fire them at the English.'

'The more men, the better. Let's see how well these rockets perform in war. There's no time to lose, Lutf Ali. We need to intercept the English before they get close to Madras.'

Hyder's army quickly moved after Colonel Wood and caught up with him just outside Vellore, where the colonel was forced into battle. Hyder's forces occupied a ridge while Colonel Wood's army stood at the bottom of the ridge. The armies were in formation on both sides, raring to fight. The English, who had fewer cavalry, employed their standard tactic – a tight square formation with the stronger and more valuable troops and artillery on the inside and the musketry on the outside.

'Lutf Ali, unleash the rockets. Get the men with the rockets to attack the centre of the square.'

Lutf Ali Beg got the men in position. Unlike the conventional formation where soldiers would be close together, the men were positioned far apart, lest the fire they used accidently light up the other rockets, causing havoc within their own ranks. The new rockets had larger iron cans, sturdier bamboo sticks and a sword dipped in oil attached to the can. The men lit up the swords, stuck the rockets in the ground and got ready to fire.

'Light the fuses!'

The men lit the fuses and moved back. There was hissing and crackling as the fuses burnt. The firing wasn't synchronous. The rockets took off in a haphazard fashion, some exploding on the spot, while the rest shot up in all directions. But the high-pitched noise was terrifying; it startled the horses and scared the English sepoys. They had never heard anything like this before. Some of the rockets did reach their intended destination – the English formation. Flaming swords rained down from the sky and slashed every man and beast in their path. One of these swords hit Colonel Wood on the shoulder, and such was the impact that he immediately collapsed to the ground. He was not dead but was bleeding profusely. But he had not given up yet. He ordered his men, 'Hold the formation! Don't yield!'

These were English sepoys, and none of them retreated seeing their commander almost mortally wounded. They stood steady but a part of the formation was broken because of the casualties. This was the chance Hyder had been waiting for. 'Kuzzaks! Through the gap! Charge!'

The kuzzaks rushed down the ridge against the English. The sepoys were unwaveringly calm. They got their muskets in position and fired at the charging kuzzaks. Many men fell under their horses, but there were too many of them, and they swarmed one part of the square, breaking it and killing as many sepoys as possible. Once the kuzzak wave had accomplished its purpose, they retreated to their positions.

Meanwhile, the Mysore musketeers had moved forward such that the English soldiers were in their range. With the retreat of the cavalry, they started their barrage of shots against the square. More men fell but the English stood their ground. They regrouped once more to form a smaller square. But they did not have a strong cavalry to take on the advancing musketry. All the while, Colonel Wood was bleeding on the ground.

An English captain knew that there would be a massacre if they didn't retreat. But Hyder had moved his troops to cover all exit points. The captain then had an idea. He sent some men on to the opposite ridge with a secret message. As the second wave of the kuzzaks bore down on them, these men climbed up the ridge and started shouting, 'Colonel Smith! Colonel Smith!' waving the English colours.

Hyder saw the men on the ridge. He yelled, 'Colonel Smith's men are on the way. We cannot fight a two-front battle. Order the men to retreat!' The Mysore army quickly moved to safer ground, leaving the wounded English to themselves.

The ruse had worked. The Mysore army had left them alone, and the now much-thinned-out English rushed to Madras to ensure the safety of Colonel Wood. However, the English in Madras wouldn't give up. They tried to open another front on the southwestern border of Mysore at Karur. Hyder Ali's stamina was undiminished too. He changed direction yet again and brought his army to Vaniambadi near Karur. The English had already taken over the fort.

It was now time for Hyder's French contingent to show their prowess. Hyder ordered them to have the cannons target a weak spot in the fort. Firing began in earnest, and soon the wall was breached. He ordered his French companies to capture the walls and gates of the fort.

The English garrison was small, but they offered a spirited defence along the ramparts. The French soldiers eventually overcame the resistance and captured the fort. Many English soldiers and the commandant of the fort were taken prisoners.

After the fort had been secured, Hyder arrived to take stock of the situation. A small court was set up and Hyder commanded, 'Bring the English prisoners.'

The officers and soldiers were put in chains and then separated. The soldiers were paraded around the fort while the officers were brought forward.

Hyder was surprised when he noticed the commandant of the English force in chains. He had a shaggy red beard. His hair was ruffled and his red coat couldn't hide his bloodstains. But Hyder's keen eyes didn't betray him. He asked, 'Colonel Nixon? Didn't we meet in Kaveripuram last year?'

Colonel Nixon kept his head down and didn't reply.

'I remember taking you as prisoner there as well. I also remember you making me a promise.'

Colonel Nixon was still silent.

At the start of this war, when the English had made their first stand against Hyder Ali at Kaveripuram, Colonel Nixon had been the commandant of the fort there. He had offered a dogged defence, stalling Hyder's progress. But they had not been able to withstand the onslaught for long. The overwhelming firepower of Mysore troops had quickly sapped the morale of the garrison and it was only a matter of time before they would have been massacred. But Colonel Nixon had sought an honourable exit from the siege.

Hyder, impressed by the bravery of the English officers, had offered a deal to them. If they gave up the fort and promised not to take up arms against Mysore for the remaining course of the war, he would set them free. He had specifically spoken to Colonel Nixon, asking him to surrender his weapons and stay away from warfare. Colonel Nixon had promised to do so and all his men were given a safe passage out of the fort. Now, months later, Hyder stood in front of the colonel, who had once again taken up arms and stood against Mysore.

Hyder loathed men who didn't keep their word. He looked at Colonel Nixon menacingly, 'Let me refresh your memory. You begged for your life and all I asked in return was for you to retire and never fight again. Do you remember your promise?' Hyder had no intention of waiting for Colonel Nixon's reply. 'Imprison them all! Send them in chains to Srirangapatna.'

The English's attempt to open a new front was foiled by Hyder again. Now that he was here, he decided to recruit more men and raise money and supplies by extracting tributes from the palegars. This went on for weeks while the English replaced Colonel Wood with Colonel Lang who, unlike his predecessor, decided to take up a defensive position instead of mounting an offensive attack on Hyder.

With additional troops, supplies and money, Hyder marched back to Vellore. He dispatched Lutf Ali Beg and Tipu to take over all the forts captured by the English. The strategy remained the same – leave a light garrison in the fort and move towards Madras.

Most of these forts were held by Wallajah's men, who capitulated in no time. Things were finally moving in the direction Hyder desired. All the forts and strategic points on the way to Madras were now in his control. He took a brief reprieve before making a final move towards the English capital. He held court in his war tent with his generals. He said, 'Lutf Ali, I see potential in the rockets. You need them to be more accurate. If executed correctly, they'll cause terror in the enemies' hearts.'

'I am already working on it, my lord. We will have rockets with better precision in the future.'

'Good!'

Hyder was then told that a letter had arrived from the nizam. One of the scribes read out the contents. The nizam had enquired whether he needed any assistance and assured him that Hyderabad will always be there to help him. 'The nizam believes that I am unaware of his cowardice and betrayal. I should have never trusted him. I know his words are empty. Ask him to retire to Hyderabad. I will handle the English myself.'

As Hyder pushed forward towards Madras, a pitched battle began between Colonel Lang and Hyder Ali, with no one getting a decisive advantage. But the tide of war was moving in Hyder's favour, albeit slowly. He was finally a couple of days away from Madras. Calling on his son, he ordered, 'Tipu, take your cavalry and attack the English until I bring the entire army near their fort.'

St Thomas Mount was a small church around ten kilometres from the port of Madras, frequented by Christian missionaries. It was a sanctuary, far away from the war taking place in the plains between the English and the Mysore state.

Tipu's horses arrived in the evening, shattered the peace and quiet of the place. They set the few hay huts built around the church on fire and chased the missionaries into the Madras Fort. Tipu wanted the English to know that the Mysore army had arrived. He set up camp near the church and waited for his father.

Alarm bells rang through the administration in Madras. War had finally come home. The Governor of Madras feared for his life. The armies in Bengal and Bombay would take weeks to reach him, and the entire Mysore army was outside the fort. He had to do something.

The bulk of the Mysore army arrived near Madras in the next few days and set up camp. Hyder was in his tent with his generals. 'I don't want to defeat the English,' he said. 'The last thing I want is to face the larger Bengal and Bombay armies. I want friendship with them. They will make powerful allies. I have seen them in battle. Of all the enemies we have faced, they will be the pre-eminent force in these lands in no time. It's better to have them as our friends. Let's wait for them to initiate a peace offering.'

As expected, the English sent two ambassadors to Hyder Ali's camp. They proposed the reversion of territories and an exchange of prisoners. They had offered nothing in return, but Hyder had the upper hand. He asked for a formal treaty between the two powers. The English had only two options – it was either a treaty or the siege of Madras.

The treaty Hyder drafted set up an offensive and defensive alliance between the English and Mysore. The two parties would not attack each other, and if one party got into a conflict with any of the major powers in the region, then the other party was obliged to come to its aid. In return, Hyder agreed to both of their terms. Fearing for their lives, the English hastily signed the treaty, and peace had been established in the region.

Hyder saw this as a major victory. He was able to make an alliance with the English on his own terms. He had proved that he could take on a technologically superior force and emerge victorious. With a satisfied heart and mind, he returned home.

Back in Srirangapatna, Hyder had to tackle another major challenge: his son's wedding, which turned out to be an excruciating exercise. He sat talking to Fatima in her zenana. 'Tipu will be married into a family of pious men. We come from a family of pious men. This man is one of the most renowned Sufi saints in Arcot. I don't understand why you are against this relationship.'

Fatima too was exasperated. 'Tipu likes Lal Mian's daughter. Lal Mian died for you during the siege of Srirangapatna. We should let Tipu marry his daughter – it's the least you can do for Lal Mian.'

'How did he get to know this girl? Has he been chasing girls instead of studying?'

'She is his favourite commander Burhan-ud-din's sister. You should allow your son to marry the girl he loves.'

'No! I have decided that Tipu will marry the daughter of the holy man and that is final.'

There was murmuring amongst the relatives, and the oldest lady spoke up. 'The pious man's family is not a good one. We have heard rumours of his uncle's escapades with the ladies of the night. How can the son of the nawab marry into such a base family?'

Hyder got angry. 'The father is a good man and his daughter is an angel. That's what matters. Who cares what his extended family is up to?'

Fatima wouldn't allow it. 'That's not how the world will look at this union. You are the Nawab of Mysore. We need our child to marry into an esteemed family. Burhan-ud-din comes from such an esteemed family. Tipu should marry his sister.'

'I want my son to marry the pious man's daughter and that's final.'

Fatima too was adamant. 'My son will marry Lal Mian's daughter.'

Hyder was the overlord of tens and thousands of soldiers; lakhs of people lived and died by his word. He was one of the most powerful men in the world and yet he could not convince his wife. He had to come to a compromise. 'All right, Tipu can marry both women.'

But Fatima had her own conditions.

'The weddings have to be on the same day then. I want the girls to have equal rights.'

'Fine!'

Fatima smiled with satisfaction. She had got what she desired. Her face turned serious again. She had important things to do now so she shooed her husband away, 'Good. Now, leave us alone. We have a lot going on.'

The weddings were a grand affair, a spectacle never seen before in Srirangapatna. Guests arrived from far and wide. The city was brightly decorated and the buildings wore a fresh coat of paint. There was music, dance and rich feasts everywhere in the city. Twenty-four-year-old Tipu, who looked like his mother right down to his aquiline nose, was decked in thick necklaces studded with precious stones and wore the finest silks of the land. With his fiery moustache and above-average height, he definitely looked like the man of the hour. After the nikkah was completed, the celebrations went on for a week. The whole city celebrated the marriage of the son of the Sultan of Mysore.

13

The end of monsoon in 1770, Srirangapatna

THE MOOD IN HYDER ALI'S COURT WAS AGITATED. THEY had faced many wars and survived to tell the tale. They had always been prudent and tactful in dealing with their adversaries, which had ensured their survival. It was this very experience that made the ministers in the Mysore court disagree with Hyder's present proposal. His revenue minister, Shamiayya, said, 'My lord, I believe paying off the Marathas is a better proposition than taking on the entire army of Peshwa Madhav Rao.'

Lutf Ali Beg concurred with Shamiayya. 'They have already crossed the Tungabhadra and are moving south. Our spies say that they have the entire cavalry and artillery with them. This is not the right time to take them on!'

Shamiayya added, 'We can get the chauth from the palegars from across the kingdom. We will be able to raise the money in no time without any major impact to the treasury. Paying them off is the safer option, my lord.'

Hyder was silent as his ministers spoke.

I am tired of running away from the Marathas. It has always been about surviving against their attacks. I want to live with a free mind.

Once the ministers were done, Hyder spoke his mind, 'Peshwa Madhav Rao is adamant about punishing me. No amount of money will satisfy him now. The chauth is just a facade to disguise his anger. We haven't paid it for years. Why has he chosen to come now? Why does he need to bring his entire army when we are barely a tenth of his forces? He is determined to eliminate me. We have to meet him on the field. There is no other option.'

'We risk extermination if we stand up against them.'

'We have to stand up to the peshwa one day or another. It just so happens that we have chosen to defy him when their entire army is against us. Let's focus on surviving this attack rather than arguing if we should fight them all. Tell me, what are the options when we face them?'

Mohammed Ali spoke up, 'We have to fight a war of attrition. We will have to wear them through constant attacks. They have a lot of supplies and camp followers. We need to focus our attacks on them. Cut their supplies, have them chase us until they tire. We can cut down on our armour to increase our speed and evade their pursuits.'

'That will not be enough, Mohammed Ali. Scorch the earth in their path. Poison all the wells, burn every field. They should not be able to feed off the land. Take no prisoners. I want to end the Maratha menace one way or the other. We have been cowering in fear for far too long.'

The kuzzaks shed their armour and went after the slow-moving Maratha juggernaut at lightning speed. They slashed and burned all the fields along the way. Every well was poisoned. Villagers were forced out of their homes to other locations, lest they were hired by the Marathas for foraging, or were looted. During their entire operation, the kuzzaks ensured that they did not encounter the main Maratha army.

Despite the obstacles that were being put up by the kuzzaks, the Maratha army moved deeper and deeper into Mysore.

The light cavalry of Mysore went behind the Maratha lines, hoping to cut off the supply chain. But they met with a surprise – there was no supply chain. The Marathas knew Hyder Ali's tactics. They had come with supplies for the long haul. So, they did not need to forage, they didn't get any camp followers and didn't have any dependencies. They had taken precautions against all exigencies. Their march to Srirangapatna continued apace. Slowly and steadily, they drew closer and closer.

In Srirangapatna, the Mysore army was getting ready. Mohammed Ali was with Hyder. He said, 'We will challenge them at Melukote. There are enough exits for us if things go wrong. Are you sure we shouldn't take the artillery with us, my lord?'

'No, just the cavalry, musketry and the men with the rockets. We need to steer the Marathas away from the capital. That's our objective. No supplies, no artillery, no slow-moving people with us. We will attack them and retreat north when they chase us.'

The army moved out of the gates and marched north to intercept the Marathas. As soon as the Maratha scouts informed Peshwa Madhav Rao about Hyder Ali's movements, the former ordered his artillery into formation.

Hyder was shocked to see the size of the Maratha forces. 'It seems that they have brought all of their artillery. They have covered the horizon with their cannons. Split the cavalry and go to the extreme ends. Have the musketry retreat to higher ground. We will need them when their army moves forward. Mohammed Ali, take the left flank. Tipu will take the right.'

The kuzzaks were split into two groups and sent in opposite directions to flank the Marathas. No sooner had the kuzzaks got in range of the cannons than the Marathas started firing at the incoming cavalry. No matter how wide the horsemen went, the cannons changed direction accordingly to attack them. Eventually, the Mysore cavalry were driven out of the field.

With the horses out of action, the peshwa ordered the bulk of his cavalry to move forward and attack Hyder. They outnumbered Hyder's forces by more than ten to one. The nawab didn't even have enough shots to kill them all. He had to make the best use of his rockets to scare away the cavalry. 'Rockets! Move forward! In position!'

The camels carrying ammunition also moved forward along with the rocket-bearing men. But before these men could take their positions, a Maratha cannon ball hit a camel, lighting up the ammunition. The fire had a cascading effect as the camel fell on the other camels and all the ammunition exploded, killing the men. Now Hyder was left without his rockets, ammunition *and* men.

He had to make a quick decision. After a few volleys from his musketry, he ordered a retreat into the thorny shrub forest. Knowing the terrain well, he was able to hide quickly, He was safe ... for now. But he had failed in his endeavour to halt the Maratha progress to the capital of Mysore. Hyder decided it was time for a full retreat.

Seeing the Mysore army retreating into the forest, Peshwa Madhav Rao heaved a sigh of relief.

The Mysore army has been defeated. My objective is finally nearing completion.

He called his war council, consisting of his generals including his relatives, Trimuk Rao and Morari Rao. 'We have nearly defeated Hyder Ali and should not cut him any slack now. We need to go straight to Srirangapatna. Nanjaraja Wodeyar has helped us a lot in this campaign. I want to see him installed as the true ruler of Mysore.' Everyone concurred with the peshwa.

'Unfortunately, I will not be able to accompany you. My campaign against Hyder Ali for all these years has taken a toll on my health. I want to return home.'

There was murmuring in the council. They were very close to decimating Hyder Ali and the peshwa was talking of going home.

Peshwa Madhav Rao sensed their disagreement. He knew he had to give more details to his men. In a sober voice, the peshwa said, 'I have *raja yakshma*.'

The entire tent plunged into despair. Everyone was stunned to hear about the Peshwa's disease. If one contracted tuberculosis, death was the only way out. The peshwa didn't want to alarm his men further. 'We all know that there is no cure. I want to spend my last days in Poona with my wife. I have spent more time pursuing this man than I have spent with my family. My heart yearns to be with her in my last days. My life goal of defeating Hyder Ali is almost achieved. It is indeed my misfortune that I cannot be there the day Hyder Ali is finally crushed. But I have brought the Maratha army this close, and now I want you to complete this task for me. Trimuk Rao will take over the army and lead it to Srirangapatna and conquer it for the Marathas.'

Peshwa Madhav Rao and his guards turned towards Poona the very next day.

In the Mysore camp, Hyder, depressed by his defeat, had taken to drinking. Mohammed Ali had arrived late in the evening following their retreat and went straight to the tent of the nawab.

A heavily drunk Hyder said, 'I have no answer to the Marathas. I thought I had the best army in the land. I now know that my army is filled with cowards and peasants. Even the peasants are better than you lot.'

Mohammed Ali knew that it was better to remain silent and wait till Hyder had completely exhausted his anger. 'Are you the famed kuzzaks? You ran away from a bunch of cannons. A disgrace! That's what you are – a disgrace! Nothing more!'

Just as his anger reached a crescendo, a commander arrived and said excitedly, 'My lord, Tipu has arrived in the camp. He is safe and sound.'

'That imbecile has finally come back! I trusted him with the cavalry, and he couldn't even find his way back after we retreated. He will bring shame to my name. Get me my whip!'

An alarmed Mohammed Ali said, 'My lord, he is your son. We have all disgraced you in equal measure. Tipu was brave during his encounter with the Marathas. It was not Tipu's fault.'

'Quiet, Mohammed Ali.'

A page retrieved a whip and gave it to Hyder as Tipu walked into his father's camp. Hyder staggered out in a drunken stupor, his eyes red. Without warning, he snapped his whip on Tipu's hand. Tipu fell, wincing in pain.

'You call yourself the son of Hyder? You are a disgrace to my name! You can't handle a bunch of pindaris, you inept fool!'

The whip lashed his son's back. Soon, Tipu lay motionless. Mohammed Ali immediately rushed to shield the boy. 'Please forgive him, my lord. We have greater blame than Tipu. Please punish us, but spare your son.'

Having exhausted his anger, Hyder threw down the whip and went back to his tent. Mohammed Ali picked up the boy and sent him to his tent. Hakeems were sent to Tipu to tend to the wounds.

Hyder finally went to sleep, and Mohammed Ali took it upon himself to address the largest concern in the camp. He called in his commanders and said, 'We need to break camp before dawn and retreat to Srirangapatna. We are too close to the Marathas. Sleep light and in a few hours, we will move as discreetly as possible. We don't want to let the Marathas know we're retreating.'

Hyder slept through the night, and no one dared to wake him up. The camp waited to move. Finally, when Hyder woke up, he saw Mohammed Ali waiting outside his tent. Hyder was back to his normal self. He called Mohammed Ali over and said, 'We need to leave as soon as possible. Staying here any longer could be dangerous.'

'We are ready, my lord. We are only waiting for your order.'

'Begin the retreat.'

The camp had already been broken up and the soldiers started moving out. But lack of sleep through the night had its consequences. A sleepy soldier accidentally let off his musket. The sound reverberated through the dry forest, waking up all the birds in the trees.

Morari Rao, the commandant of Gooty, who had once been held prisoner by Hyder, had camped nearby. He was one of the chief generals of the peshwa in this invasion. The shot rung in his ear.

'Hyder Ali is nearby. Get the cavalry! We need to corner him now!'

The army under Morari Rao galloped through the forest. The Mysore army realized that they were being chased and they marched towards the capital at full speed. A running battle soon ensued between the two. The slower Mysore troops, especially the musketry, eventually stopped for a last stand against the Marathas. With almost no ammunition, the infantry were broken by the Maratha cavalry with ease. The faster but panicked troops with Hyder could not outrun the Maratha horses and they scattered in all directions.

Hyder and his guards finally reached a water tank. A personal guard looked up to his master and said, 'We can't outrun the Marathas for long, my lord. We need you to reach Srirangapatna safely. I will disguise myself as you and let the Marathas capture me. You can disguise yourself as a soldier and reach the capital. No one will chase ordinary horsemen.'

There was no time for arguing. Hyder embraced his bodyguard in gratitude, switched clothes with him and took his ring to identify himself with his family. For this supreme sacrifice, Hyder would ensure that his bodyguard's family was taken care of. He made away from the tank.

Morari Rao himself came to the tank with his cavalry. He had never seen Hyder Ali before but he recognized the clothes, the all-white cotton outfit from the top to the bottom, the yellow cummerbund around his waist, the yellow turban and a body devoid of jewellery. The Sultan of Mysore was known for his simple clothes and lack of fascination for anything fancy, delicate or expensive. Everyone near the tank was captured.

Under the impression that Hyder had been captured by them, the Marathas changed their plan. They decided to go to the temple in Melukote. Having heard about the riches of this temple, they decided to plunder it before going to Srirangapatna. Who would defend the capital now that Hyder was their prisoner?

Lutf Ali Beg, who was guarding the fort of Srirangapatna, was the first to recognize Hyder despite his disguise. The small group of horses was quickly let inside the fort.

Hyder had only one question for Lutf Ali Beg, 'Where is my son? Is he safe?'

'I don't know, my lord. You are the first to arrive.'

Tears welled up in Hyder's eyes but he quickly steeled himself. 'Prepare the defences. The Marathas will be here soon. We must be ready for a long siege. Get as many supplies and men inside as you can.'

'Yes, my lord.'

The next day, Mohammed Ali and some of his men arrived in tattered clothes at the gates of Srirangapatna.

Hyder was anxious as he asked, 'Mohammed Ali, have you seen Tipu?'

'No, my lord. We were ambushed by the Marathas and we barely made it out alive. Tipu was not with us.'

Hyder's heart sunk further. Mohammed Ali, together with Lutf Ali Beg, went about preparing the defences of the city. Hyder stood in the bastion of the fort looking at the horizon, waiting for his son.

I shouldn't have beaten him. The last thing I did to my son was hit him. He is the one person I loved with all my heart and now I have lost him.

Hyder wept as the evening sun sank below the horizon. Every day for an entire week, he came to the bastion, looking far into the forest, hoping his son would turn up. He lost interest in the defence of the city. A few days later, some pindaris appeared out of the forest and raced towards the gate. Fearing that these were the scouts for the Marathas, the musketry immediately took aim.

'Wait! Don't shoot! Don't shoot! That's my son!'

Hyder rushed from the bastion and ordered the gates to be opened. He took his horse and galloped towards the pindaris. 'Tipu! Tipu!'

'Father!' Tipu, dressed as a pindari, rushed towards his father.

Hyder got off his horse and hugged his son, who had also disembarked. Tears of relief rolled down Hyder's face. He took his son by the hand and they went inside the fort.

'How did you escape from the Marathas, son?'

'My bodyguards and I escaped on foot, Father. We lay down with the dead soldiers even as the Maratha soldiers were searching each of our dead for gold. I disposed of all my gold before burying the dead. Once the Marathas left, we traced our way back. Some of the pindaris were loitering around in the forest on their horses looking for more of our dead soldiers to steal their gold. We plunged our daggers into them and used their clothes and horses to get out of the forest. Since we looked like pindaris, nobody stopped us. We made our way through a convoluted route so as to not arouse suspicion. That is why we took a long time to reach the fort, Father,'

Hyder held his son close as they walked towards the palace.

'I am just happy that you are safe, son.'

I would have never forgiven myself if I had lost you.

Now that his son was safe, the old Hyder was back. He took active interest in the defence of the citadel. Walls were strengthened. Supplies were brought in to withstand a siege that could go on for years. Having lost most of his men and horses in the retreat, he actively recruited additional men and brought them inside the fort.

While all of this was happening in Srirangapatna, Trimuk Rao and his men continued with the plunder of Melukote. Despite Peshwa Madhav Rao's desire to take Srirangapatna immediately, the Marathas spent a sizeable amount of time looting and pillaging. When they had finally finished plundering, the army marched towards Srirangapatna only to find it was prepared to withstand the siege. Nevertheless, Trimuk Rao ordered his men to begin the blockade.

A few weeks later, news arrived that Peshwa Madhav Rao had passed away. He was replaced by his younger brother, Narayan Rao. Though Madhav Rao's desire of defeating Hyder Ali remained unfulfilled, the siege of Srirangapatna continued. There was no progress for weeks. During a meeting in Hyder's court, Tipu made a suggestion, 'Father, the Marathas have grown lax. Now is our chance to steal some supplies and horses from them and augment our resources. With your permission, I will personally lead this endeavour. We will have them crying for supplies in no time.'

There was no danger to Srirangapatna and the city could withstand the siege for a year. Hyder saw minimal risk in Tipu's suggestion. 'Go ahead, attack them. If we can augment our supplies, it would be an added benefit.'

Tipu and his men made routine raids on the Maratha camp and stole supplies and horses. These guerrilla atacks went on for months. Despite these losses, Trimuk Rao stuck with the siege. After a few months, more bad news arrived at the Maratha camp. Raghunath Rao, the new peshwa's uncle, had murdered the young peshwa and taken over. But not many accepted his rule and a civil war was brewing within the Maratha Empire. Trimuk Rao was needed in Poona, but lifting the siege would be a loss of face for him and the Marathas.

News of the murder in Poona reached Hyder as well. Hyder understood Trimuk Rao's predicament. He wanted to make the best of the situation. He called his war council for a meeting. 'Trimuk Rao needs a respectable way out of the siege. I think we should offer him a tribute and release Srirangapatna from the clutches of the Marathas.'

Tipu concurred with his father, as did Lutf Ali Beg.

Hyder said, 'Send an ambassador to the Maratha camp. Offer them two lakh rupees to raise the siege.'

'Two lakhs? Wouldn't that be seen as an insult?'

'That's a choice Trimuk Rao has to make. I am willing to sit inside the capital for another year if need be. Send our ambassador.'

Trimuk Rao wanted to save face, and he knew the pittance offered by Hyder was a downright insult. But he was willing to let it go. He proclaimed that Hyder Ali's tribute was an acknowledgement that the nawab submitted to the supremacy of the Marathas. Accepting the money, the Marathas decamped from Srirangapatna and went back to face the volatile situation in Poona. After withstanding the siege for an entire year, Mysore was finally free of the Marathas.

After the last Maratha left Mysore, Hyder called Mohammed Ali for a secret meeting. 'I have found out that Nanjaraja has secretly been helping the peshwa. We can't have traitors in our midst. Please do the needful.'

It did not take more than a week for Mohammed Ali to act.

Nanjaraja Wodeyar was oblivious to the fact that his secret communication with the peshwa had been discovered by Hyder. The Mysore king, oblivious, kept up his correspondence. One morning, as was his routine, Nanjaraja Wodeyar was getting ready for his bath. He undressed and sat on a small stool. Closing his eyes, he waited for a servant to massage his body with aromatic oils and release the tension in his muscles. The servant arrived, bowed to the king and asked for permission to start the massage. The king, his eyes still closed, lazily granted permission. The man took some oil in his hands and started massaging the shoulders. The king groaned with relief as his muscles relaxed. The page slowly moved his hands above the shoulders and in a split second, he snapped the king's neck. The king fell down, motionless. The man wiped his hands on a towel and left the bathroom.

With the sudden death of Nanjaraja Wodeyar, it was time to appoint a new king of Mysore. Hyder was in the king's palace with his ministers and generals. He ordered, 'Bring all the royal children here.'

All the potential heirs of the Wodeyars were brought into the hall. They were either toddlers or little children. 'Let them come in the centre and play.'

The centre of the hall was littered with a variety of things: dolls, paper, perfume, glass toys, fruits and sweets. It was completely random. The innocent children quite happily came into the centre. Some picked up toys to play with while some picked up sweets to eat and others just sat down. A toddler looked around and walked to a pillar nearby. He squatted and picked up a dagger.

Hyder smiled. 'That's our king. What is the name of the boy?'

'Chamaraja Wodeyar, my lord.'

'Chamaraja Wodeyar will be the new king. Prepare for the coronation. Move the boy and his family to the palace.'

While the preparations for the coronation were underway, Hyder told Mohammed Ali, 'Morari Rao is back in Gooty.

He is the scoundrel who nearly killed me near Melukote. I can't let his actions go unpunished.'

'We are ready to march on your command, my lord.'

'What are we waiting for? Let's move to Gooty.'

Once the coronation ceremony had been completed, Hyder marched to the province of Gooty that bordered the nizam's territory. On reaching the town below the Gooty fort, they were surprised to find it empty. The fort on top was heavily garrisoned with Morari Rao's men, and Morari Rao himself was holed up there. After occupying the town, Hyder's men besieged the fort. He did not offer any terms for surrender. He followed his usual tactics – communication with the outside world was cut off, no supplies came in or went out. Morari Rao and his men were completely isolated.

Hyder ordered, 'Send in some spies. I want to know the situation in the fort. Morari Rao seems to be quite confident about the siege.'

The spies fanned out in the countryside. Soon, they were back in Hyder's camp and said, 'Morari Rao has brought the whole town inside the fort. While they have large amounts of supplies, there is only one tank of water. If we prolong the siege till summer and if the summer is intense, we will have the fort without firing a single shot.'

Happy with the news, Hyder decided to continue the siege. With the advent of summer, a peace offering came from Morari Rao. The writer read out the proposal to Hyder, 'He is willing to offer ten lakh rupees in cash and vacate the fort if you assure the safety of his family.'

'There's no need to reply to this offer. I will wait for him to die of thirst.'

Within a month, Morari Rao left the fort with his followers and came to the Mysore camp. He was apprehended and brought in chains to Hyder.

Hyder Ali was in no mood to listen to Morari Rao. He ordered his generals, 'I don't want to see his face. Take him to Srirangapatna and put him back in prison. Every one of his followers will suffer the same fate. I hope the prison will consume him this time.'

The end of summer, 1774, Srirangapatna

Hyder laughed hysterically. 'Why would I pay him? Who does he think he is? All the Marathas are against him. Even help from the English will not save him. We all know about the promises and treaties made by the English. They didn't help me in my hour of need. I don't think they will help him either.'

'What about his offer to cede the land between the Tungabhadra and the Krishna to us?'

'Let's take it. But that doesn't guarantee that I will pay him. He is ceding territory to everyone. Even the English got some. He is trying everything to hold on to the seat of the peshwa. It is a lost cause. He is on his own now. I have already received a letter from Nana Fadnavis in Poona warning me not to support Raghunath Rao.'

Raghunath Rao, after killing his nephew, had taken over as the peshwa. But not everyone had accepted his suzerainty. Nana Fadnavis, a powerful minister in the Maratha court, was leading the rebellion against him. In order to acquire more support, Raghunath Rao had come south of the Tungabhadra to collect more troops from the strongholds of the Marathas in the south. During this time, he offered the plains between the rivers Tungabhadra and Krishna to Hyder Ali in return for financing his campaign against Nana Fadnavis.

Hyder knew that Nana Fadnavis had the upper hand. There was no love lost between him and the Marathas. He wanted to make the most of this. Taking Raghunath Rao at his word, he took his army and crossed the Tungabhadra to defeat the Maratha territory. The first stop was the capital of the province – Dharwad.

The commandant of the fort refused to surrender, saying that he was loyal to Nana Fadnavis and not Raghunath Rao. Hyder was in a quandary. He had already entered Maratha territory, and he knew that he had antagonized the Marathas again. He decided to make the best of the situation. He decided to capture Dharwad.

Hyder had just finished eating when he heard gunshots. He rushed out of his tent to see Mohammed Ali's musketry firing at a small Maratha force that had come to Dharwad's rescue. The musketry was intense and, sensing defeat, the Maratha forces moved towards the fort. The commandant of the fort too sensed the impeding defeat and opened the gates to allow the Maratha soldiers inside. The Mysore musketry withdrew while the cavalry chased them before retreating as well.

Hyder ordered Mohammed Ali to his presence to deliver a report of the incident.

'Our plan has worked! The commandant has taken in our troops. We just fired blanks at each other.'

'Well done, Mohammed Ali. Have your troops ready to go inside. I want the whole operation to be complete by dawn.'

The plan worked like clockwork. The Mysore soldiers who had got inside the fort disguised as the Marathas opened the gates in the dead of the night and Mohammed Ali's troops quickly captured the gates and bastions. The fort soon fell to the Mysore troops.

After sanitizing the fort, Hyder carried out a thorough inspection of the state of affairs. 'Who was leading our Maratha decoys?'

'Purniah, my lord. He is one of your accountants.'

'An accountant? I must be more careful when it comes to my accountants. You know about Khande Rao?'

Mohammed Ali was quick to vouch for his man. 'I will personally vouch for Purniah. He is a great asset for Mysore.'

'Well, that's good to hear. Take Purniah and your other commanders and clean up the remaining Maratha forts and towns in the region.'

The bulk of the Mysore army went to capture all the forts in the region including Koppal, Badami and Gajendragad. All of them surrendered and the control of these forts passed on to Mysore. As they were being cleaned up, Tipu had important news for his father.

'Father, the nizam's Bellary Fort does not have a garrison. It is just a day's march from here. Shall we take the nizam's fort?'

'What's stopping us?'

'Nothing, Father. But our activities here have caught the attention of the nizam. He is sending some troops to reinforce Bellary. We will need to move quickly.'

'Go ahead then. There is no time to lose.'

Tipu took his army and marched towards Bellary. Speed was of the essence. It was a rapid march and the empty fort was easily taken. After a few days, the huge army of the nizam turned up near Bellary. Tipu decided to put his artillery and rockets to good use. He ordered his cannons and rockets into formation. His cannons had much longer range than the ones that the nizam possessed. As soon as the enemy was in range, he opened fire. The mess of a formation that was the nizam's forces soon scattered.

'Move the rockets closer to their forces and fire at them.'

The men with the rockets quickly moved forward and fired all the rockets at the infantry. All hell broke loose. The shrill noise scared the already terrified horses and the cavalry beat a hasty retreat. The infantry had never seen flaming swords raining from the sky. Fear struck their hearts and they too ran away. A small force remained on the field, a combination of cavalry and infantry. The rockets startled them but they did not run away, and they began forming a square – these were Europeans.

Tipu got the cannons to change direction and target the square. He withdrew his rocket men and got his cavalry ready. The firing started, and the square took a lot of blows but they did not yield. They started moving forward.

Tipu wasn't going to wait either. He ordered, 'Cavalry, on my command!'

Wave after wave of Mysore cavalry fell on the square. The Europeans took huge losses but held steady. Finally, Tipu had the entire cavalry attack the square.

The next day, Hyder was looking into the accounts of the treasury in Dharwad when Tipu arrived at the gates. He immediately went to Hyder's palace and said, 'Father, Bellary belongs to Mysore now. I scared and defeated the nizam's army.'

Looking up from the papers, he said, 'Well done, son. The nizam's forces were never known for their bravery. A good scare has them retreating in no time.'

'Well, actually, the French forces under the nizam put up a commendable resistance.'

Hyder looked up. Tipu continued, 'I was impressed by them and after they were defeated, I decided to hire them into our forces.'

'What is the name of their commander?'

'Lally.'

'What's his rank?'

'He's a mercenary and not associated with the French army.'

'You hired a mercenary who used to work for the nizam, and who gladly left the nizam's pay to join you. How are you sure he will be loyal to you, Tipu?'

'I offered him a steady pay and adventure. I trust him, Father.'

Hyder sighed.

'You are old enough to make these decisions. As my general, you can keep him and his men on your payroll.'

The capture of all the lands up to the Krishna river evoked predictable reactions from the Marathas and the nizam. The two powers formed an alliance and declared war on Hyder Ali. Their combined army came down south to meet the nawab.

For Hyder, there was nothing surprising about this. He had sent all the money from his recent conquests into the Dharwad treasury. He had dispatched spies and secret emissaries to many Maratha generals, to bribe them into staying away from the war. He had made all preparations to set up a camp on a strong ground near the banks of the Tungabhadra. He was, in short, completely ready for them.

This time, his secret emissaries came back with good news. One of the Maratha generals, Baarbhai, was willing to not fight in the battle for a large sum. Hyder immediately sent a letter assuring that the payment would be made soon. Things were finally falling into place.

The invading army had already crossed the Krishna and marched to the Tungabhadra to face Hyder's forces. Trimuk Rao was leading this force. He had also received news that one of his chief generals had betrayed him to Hyder Ali. He was more worried about who the turncoat was than about facing the Nawab of Mysore.

Hyder got some of his kuzzaks to come forward. 'Signal the general in our pay.'

'What do we signal?'

'Anything. I just want Trimuk Rao to know the traitor in his fold.'

A small number of kuzzaks went ahead towards Baarbhai and made some random signals. They made sure Trimuk Rao saw them. Baarbhai developed cold feet and started withdrawing his forces, and Trimuk Rao found his traitor. He immediately ordered his cavalry to fall upon the defector. The whole Maratha cavalry fell on its own, and a fight ensued.

Nizam Mir Ali Khan Asaf Jah and his army, meanwhile, were standing idle in their corner, watching the fight that had broken out within the Maratha ranks. The nizam called his generals, 'If our strongest ally is fighting amongst themselves, then I don't think we can take on the wily Hyder Ali. God knows he definitely has something up his sleeve to break up my army as well. We need to retreat before things get worse.'

The nizam's forces promptly left.

Hyder and his forces waited, watching the action unfold within the enemies' ranks.

Trimuk Rao too lost the nerve to fight Hyder. He didn't trust his own men, and the nizam had also retraced his steps. Fearing something else would go wrong, he immediately ordered a retreat to Poona. Hyder Ali was finally the master of all the lands between the two rivers –

Krishna and Tungabhadra. Despite all the setbacks and enemies swarming around him, he had expanded his empire even further at the expense of both the nizam and the Marathas.

14

1777, post harvest, Dharwad

KRISHNAPPA, THE PALEGAR OF RAYADURGA, WAS EXCITED. Hyder Ali had granted him audience. He felt that the rich tributes that he had offered the nawab had finally paid off.

Dressed in the finest of Burhanpur cotton, the clean-shaven Krishnappa didn't look out of place amongst the nobles who were standing in front of Hyder's masand. He had dabbed himself with a liberal amount of attar from Hyderabad, and the aroma hung thick in the air. He clearly wanted to be the centre of attention. He was the first in line to be addressed by the Sultan of Mysore.

Hyder, who was holding court in Dharwad, asked, 'Yes, Krishnappa, what brings you all the way from Rayadurga?'

'My lord, I know you are punishing all the palegars who went against you during the Maratha invasion. As your loyal subject, I would like to offer my assistance. I don't have many men to offer, but I have some intelligence that would be useful. Madakari Nayaka, the palegar of Chitradurga, provided men and money to the Marathas for their battle with you at Melukote. You may also be aware that he did not provide you any money or men for your last battle against the Marathas on the banks of the Tungabhadra. He is not loyal to you, and I have proof. I have intercepted the letters he had sent to the Marathas pledging his allegiance to them during the battle at Tungabhadra.'

Hyder perused the letters presented by Krishnappa. 'Thank you for the information, Krishnappa. The palegar will be taught a lesson. Give the palegar of Rayadurga gold and precious stones. He is a loyal subject of Nawab Hyder Ali.'

Krishnappa's job was done. A decades-old enmity with Madakari Nayaka, who should have known better than to oppose Krishnappa's family, would end now. No one could survive Krishnappa's wrath. If everything went well, he could even end up as the palegar of Chitradurga.

Hyder's generals had already fanned out across the kingdom extracting pending tributes and paishkash and putting down all those who had opposed the nawab during his battles against the Marathas. Hyder decided to go to Chitradurga to demand the pending tribute and, if needed, to punish any previous transgressions.

Chitradurga was one of the strongest forts in Mysore, and seven layers of walls at different levels made a siege an impossible task. It was nicknamed the 'Iron Fort' by the locals. Madakari Nayaka was a brave man, controlling the vast province around Chitradurga. Hyder was no stranger to this fact. He went in with a sizeable army.

He arrived with his troops at the gates of the great fort, and Madakari Nayaka understood that Hyder Ali had caught on to his double game. He refused the nawab entry, and this confirmed Krishnappa's accusations. Hyder besieged the Chitradurga fort. There was no peshwa or nizam around to interfere with Hyder's internal affairs this time. There were no refractory palegars in the vicinity to rally against him. Madakari Nayaka and his men were on their own.

The siege went on for three months. The palegar was holed up at the top of the hill where no rockets could reach. The walls of the fort were so thick that even intense firing could not breach them. The brave men in the fort, risking their lives, would repair the damaged walls before Hyder could begin another round of firing.

Hyder started getting impatient. 'How much longer can this go on? There are limits to bravery, and this is madness. He will soon starve to death. I need to relieve him of this misfortune. Get the infantry ready. We will storm the fort.'

The infantry was soon prepared to scale the fort. On Hyder's orders, they moved forward with ladders. Shielding themselves from the musket shots that were being fired from the bastions, they mounted the ladders against the walls. Soldiers quickly climbed up and made it onto the ramparts. But Madakari Nayaka would not give up that easily. His men were ready on the ramparts and as the Mysore soldiers climbed up, they were attacked and pushed down.

They offered stiff resistance to the scores of soldiers who kept climbing up. This went on and on, more and more soldiers died, until finally, the defenders gained the upper hand and pushed the ladders down. All of Hyder's men who had scaled the walls had fallen and this was just the first layer – there were six more before they reached the top. Hyder realized he would not be able to storm the fort. Cutting his losses, he called back his infantry.

But he did not raise the siege, instead he ordered more men to join him from the capital. Mohammed Ali and his troops arrived soon but the siege continued with no progress. It had been almost a year when Hyder was visited by some unexpected guests in his tent.

'We are Rangappa and Thimanna, the brothers-in-law of Madakari Nayaka, my lord. Our sister is married to him. We come here seeking justice,' one of them said.

'Tell me how I can help,' said Hyder.

'Our father, who used to live with us inside the fort, had visited the local deity in Rayadurga some time ago. Suspecting him of being in touch with you, Madakari Nayaka assassinated him on his return. Our father was an honest man. Now, Madakari Nayaka suspects us as well and has banished us from the fort. We have nowhere to go. We seek justice. Our father's soul will not rest in peace until Madakari Nayaka pays for his sins.'

'I have besieged Madakari Nayaka for nearly a year now. What more can I do for you?'

'We can help you, my lord. We lived inside the Chitradurga Fort for a long time. There is a secret passage which takes you inside the fort across five walls. The palegar uses this passage for all emergency supplies and stores. We can help you find the passage.'

This opportunity had come out of the blue, and Hyder immediately latched on to it. He said, 'Take our soldiers to this secret passage, and help them enter the fort. If the fort falls, I promise you, the palegar will pay for all his sins.'

The operation was planned for the night. The infantry followed the men close to the wall. Hidden amongst the bushes was a small gap just about big enough for one man to go through.

Thimanna said, pointing to the small gap, 'This is the secret entrance to the fort. Get in quickly before they discover us.'

The Mysore infantry trickled in. Some of the soldiers went up to the higher reaches while others went below. Finally, all of them were inside. When they received the signal to proceed, they struck at the fort's guards with full force. A two-front battle began inside the fort with one group fighting in the upper reaches, and another fighting the troops on the lower walls. After a brutal fight, the Mysore infantry overpowered all the soldiers on the rampart and opened the main gates.

Hyder ordered the remainder of his infantry and the cavalry to flood the fort. Soon, most of the fort's defenders had breathed their last fighting against the far superior forces of Mysore. By dawn, Chitradurga had been taken by the nawab's forces.

Hyder was still in his tent when Madakari Nayaka and his family were brought in chains. Emerging from his tent, he saw defiance in the eyes of the palegar. He asked, 'What do you have to say for yourself?'

'You may have captured my fort, but I will never bow to you!'

'So be it. Throw him off the cliff right away. Nobody should be able to find a single unbroken bone in his body. Send his family to the darkest dungeons in Srirangapatna. The rats should have a feast on the flesh of his kin.'

Madakari Nayaka was dragged away as he railed against Hyder Ali. His family too was quickly bundled away. Mohammed Ali came to Hyder, and the nawab sighed and said, 'I don't know who is loyal to me. I never thought I'd have to fight my own people. All I sought in life was freedom from the Marathas. When I am near my goal, I have to get my hands dirty fighting against people whom I called my own. But disloyal men must be punished. There is no other way.'

'There are no more disloyal men in your kingdom, my lord. They have all been sent to the next world. If you seek further retribution, there are the Pathan nawabs of Kurnool and Kadapa who sided with the nizam during our war with them near Tungabhadra.'

'I have a weakness for Pathan horses. These horses are of the highest pedigree and they will be a valuable addition to my army. The Pathans are brave on the battlefield as well. At least for the horses, I seek the friendship of the Pathans. But these Afghans are a stubborn lot. They don't want to feel the warmth of my friendship.'

Hyder looked resigned.

Is it me? Is it because I am not of high birth that these people don't accept my offer of friendship? There is no respect or honour for a kinder Hyder Ali. They only recognize the merciless Sultan of Mysore.

He acquiesced to Mohammed Ali's proposal.

'Let's move to Kadapa and Kurnool. If they answer to the language of the sword, so be it.'

The Mysore army marched east to the nominal feudatories of the nizam – Kurnool and Kadapa. Fatima's brother, Mir Sahib, held a jagir in this region. He had kept to himself during most of Hyder's campaign against the Marathas, and Hyder himself never sought any help from him. After dealing with several disloyal men, he decided to test his brother-in-law's loyalty. His first stop was at his jagir.

Mir Sahib welcomed the nawab warmly, offering him a fine choice of clothes and precious stones.

Hyder said, 'Mir Sahib, I am here to punish the nawabs of Kurnool and Kadapa for supporting the nizam during his campaign with me. Your jagir is close to their land. How can you help me?'

'Your enemies are my enemies, my lord. My men are ready to fight for you. I will also provide you with the necessary supplies for your campaign. We know the terrain well and can guide you to the two provinces and help with setting up your camp at the strongest place.'

'Good, Mir Sahib. Have your men take the forward guard position and guide my troops to Kurnool. I will use your jagir as a base during this campaign.'

Mir Sahib bowed to Hyder and took his leave.

The Mysore army was guided assiduously through the drylands by Mir Sahib and the camp was set up on strong ground, close to the Kurnool Fort. A supply chain was established from Mir Sahib's jagir to the camp. Hyder was all set to take on the Nawab of Kurnool.

The Kurnool affair was straightforward. The half-mad Pathan horsemen were blown into smithereens by the Mysore cannons. The Nawab of Kurnool was smart enough to surrender, and the province was absorbed into the ever-growing Mysore Empire. There was a new boundary between the nizam and Mysore now. As he marched towards the other Pathan province, Kadapa, Hyder told himself that this would be the last of his retributions against those who had risen against him. He was getting tired of the constant campaigns.

He set up camp north of the fort of Kadapa. Having been on the field for more than a year, he decided to rest for a while; the troops needed some respite too. He ordered the camp followers to forage for food for the horses and the soldiers.

I will let the Nawab of Kadapa, Hakeem Khan, enjoy a few more days of peace before I unleash fire and fury upon his kingdom.

The Mysore troops had gathered around campfires and were enjoying a rare day of rest. The weather was pleasant with winter setting in. The calm of the evening was broken by the sentry guards blowing their horns. 'Alert! Alert! The Pathan cavalry are coming towards to us! Alert! Alert!'

Mohammed Ali and Hyder Ali came out of their respective tents. In one voice, they cried, 'Get the cavalry moving! Intercept them!'

Both of them got into armour and on their horses. The Pathan horses had already reached the camp and started slaughtering anyone that came in their way. Unarmed camp followers and armourless foot soldiers were all cut to pieces. There was no time for formation or tactics.

'Get all our horses against them! Charge!'

Hyder Ali and Mohammed Ali personally got into the fight. In one-to-one fights, the Pathan horsemen were far superior to the Mysore horsemen. In this almost hand-to-hand fight, the Pathans had the advantage and slew many a Mysore man. But eventually, the larger Mysore cavalry got the better of the Afghans, and by nightfall, the remaining Pathan horses had retreated to Kadapa, leaving Hyder's camp in a shambles.

Taking stock of the situation, Mohammed Ali saw something good in an otherwise destroyed camp. 'Our artillery, rockets and ammunition are safe. The bulk of our cavalry are still alive and good. Our soldiers still outnumber the troops of Kadapa. We can still bring Hakeem Khan to his knees.'

Hyder, more focused on his goal than ever, said, 'Prepare the troops. Send the injured back home. We are storming Kadapa tomorrow.'

As dawn broke, the Mysore army reached the gates of Kadapa. The cannons were in position – aligned to target the gates of the fort – and the cavalry had covered the flanks while the muskets were loaded.

'Fire!' Intense shooting ensued. With only one exit from the fort, none of the Kadapa soldiers could come out. A few hours later, the gates fell. Through the dust of the broken gates, Pathan horsemen raced out. A few more cannon shots thinned the number of horses. As they came closer, Hyder ordered his musketry to open fire. Wave after wave of shots from the muskets smote everything that came in their direction. With the Kadapa cavalry decimated, the Mysore cavalry entered the fort and killed the remaining troops. The musketry then marched forward and entered Kadapa, securing all the walls of the fort. Kadapa had well and truly fallen.

Mohammed Ali was still with Hyder, watching the fort being secured. Hyder said, 'Send Hakeem Khan and his family to Srirangapatna. Capture the remaining Pathan horsemen and bring them to me. They are too useful to be killed or imprisoned.'

The rout of the Kadapa Pathans was almost absolute. Only around forty horsemen survived Hyder's attack. They were captured and brought to Hyder's camp. He told them, 'I am impressed with your bravery. Men like you should be fighting under a great name instead of these small-time nawabs. I will offer you amnesty if you choose to fight for me.'

The Pathans murmured amongst themselves. Hyder offered them the real choice then, 'Either you work for me or be killed. I would suggest you take my hand of friendship with both of your hands.' Faced with these options, the Pathans consented to work for Hyder Ali. Looking at them, he said, 'A good decision. Now, hand over your weapons to my soldiers, and you will be escorted to your tents.'

The leader of the Pathans said, 'As Pathans, we cannot hand over our weapons to our conqueror. It is a dishonour to surrender our weapons, and our honour comes before anything else. We refuse to give up our weapons.'

Mohammed Ali snapped back at them in anger, 'You either hand them over or your heads will roll this instant.'

'There's nothing to get angry about, Mohammed Ali. They just want to hold on to their weapons. They are surrounded by our troops anyway. They have pledged to work for me. I believe in their loyalty. We will allow this,' said Hyder.

A reluctant Mohammed Ali nodded his head.

'Escort these men to their tents. Mohammed Ali, you get some rest too. We will go to the fort tomorrow. It should be secure by then.'

It was a clear night with no clouds or moon in the sky. The camp was calm and quiet. It was a perfect time for the Pathans to proceed with their treachery. The forty Pathans came out of their tents and started walking silently through the camp. They were armed to the teeth and moving in the direction of Hyder's tent. This tent had two layers, with the outermost door leading to a pathway which stopped at another door, behind which were the sleeping quarters. Both the doors were manned by his personal guards.

The guards outside the tent were awake and they were the first to respond.

But the Pathans swiftly sank their swords into them and muffled their cries. However, the inner guards heard the clanking of the Pathan armour and swords. 'Alert everyone! Someone has come to assassinate the nawab!'

The Pathans outnumbered the guards, and they quickly slashed at the inner guards with their swords, killing them instantly. But the alarm had already been raised. Now the Pathans quickly rushed into Hyder's tent.

Hyder had woken up hearing the commotion outside his tent. Fearing an attack, he quickly got out of bed, put his pillows under his blanket, and using the dagger that he always kept by his side, he cut open the tent and slipped away. Just as he got out, the Afghans entered. Assuming the nawab was still in bed, they stabbed the blanket relentlessly and rushed out of the tent.

By then, the entire army was alert. They quickly cornered the Pathans and tied them up. Once they were subdued, Hyder Ali emerged from the darkness.

'You are true to your clan – there's not a drop of gratitude or loyalty in your blood. I should have kept you in your place. Chop off their hands and legs!'

His soldiers came forward and chopped off the Pathans' limbs immediately. The ground was soon soaking with blood. But Hyder was not done yet. 'Tie them to the elephants and let the animals drag them around the camp until they die.'

After a few hours, there was a path of blood running through the camp. The dismembered bodies of the Pathans were piled on a side. Hyder was sad. Mohammed Ali was with him in the partially burnt palace of Kadapa. He said to the general, 'Kadapa and Kurnool are almost finished. I don't think I will be able to source any Pathan horses from these provinces. The last Pathan nawab is in Savanur, and I can't vanquish him either. He has pledged his allegiance to me but I don't trust these Pathans anymore. I need to do something to ensure their loyalty. I am thinking of entering into a matrimonial alliance with the Nawab of Savanur. I will have my younger son Karim marry his daughter. He will then have a stronger bond with us and be less prone to treachery.'

'That's a fine idea, my lord.'

Soon after, Purniah and Mir Sahib went to Savanur with the marriage proposal. The Nawab of Savanur was a pragmatic man, and he knew the consequences of refusing Hyder Ali's proposal. He accepted it and as a part of the agreement, agreed to supply Hyder Ali with 2,000 of the finest Pathan horses when in need.

The atmosphere in Srirangapatna was jubilant in anticipation of another wedding in Hyder Ali's family. The Pathans from Savanur had arrived in the capital and were taking part in the festivities. Guests had come from across the Mysore Empire, and no expense was spared to make this wedding a lavish affair. The ambassadors of the Marathas and the nizam attended the celebrations as well. They requested a meeting with the nawab. Hyder was busy with last-minute preparations for the wedding, but the arrival of these representatives and their request for a meeting troubled him.

Apprehensive of their intentions, he immediately granted them audience in his palace. Both set of representatives insisted on meeting Hyder Ali together.

The emmisaries of the Marathas and the nizam were already present when Hyder entered his durbar. Exchanging greetings, the Maratha representative said, 'We come bearing gifts for the bridegroom and the bride. The peshwa and the nizam bless the new couple and pray for their health and progeny.'

Baskets filled with gold, silver and precious stones were presented to Hyder. He graciously accepted the gifts.

An ambassador spoke, 'Our masters have a proposition that you would be very interested in.'

A tinge of apprehension showed on Hyder's face.

'The English have been troubling us for some time now. Their support of Raghunath Rao undermines the confederacy of the Marathas. Their actions have always been against our interests. The nizam is also suffering because of the English. They have annexed his lands to create a direct land route from Bengal to Madras. Guntur is now under English control. They also actively encourage rebellions by the nizam's younger brother Basalat Jung against the nizam near Arcot. We have come to an agreement that the machinations of the English must stop. Our masters realize that there is no love lost between you and the English. Hence, we propose that you join this alliance. With our powers combined, we can eliminate the presence of the English from these lands – push them into the sea from whence they came.'

'It seems the Marathas and the nizam have serious problems with the English. I do have my own concerns with them but they are small compared to the ones you face. What would I gain by joining the alliance?'

The Maratha representative smiled. It was almost as if they were expecting this question. 'Our masters are willing to formalize the existing boundaries of Mysore. Your recent conquests will remain with you. The peshwa has agreed to reduce the annual chauth to eleven lakh rupees per year, and the nizam will renounce his claim to tributes from you.'

The likelihood of peace with the two major powers made the prospect of the alliance attractive. Hyder replied, 'Please give me some time to consult with my advisors regarding your proposal. Meanwhile, enjoy the festivities. Please convey my gratitude to your masters for the gifts.'

Hyder had a lot of commitments and spent the day handling various aspects of the wedding. It was late in the night before he could think about the rather audacious proposal put forward by the nizam and the Marathas. He called his old and sagacious general Lutf Ali Beg for a private meeting. 'The nizam and the Marathas have joined forces against the English,' said Hyder. 'They want me to join them.'

'The English are an untrustworthy lot, my lord. Despite signing a treaty of mutual assistance in Madras, they refused to help us in Melukote. It has become imperative to act against them. It's just that I am not sure if the Marathas and the nizam are the right allies.'

'That's what I was thinking as well. The nizam has already betrayed me once when we went up against the English. His army is too timid, prone to bribery and will retreat at the slightest whiff of trouble. The Marathas will turn against me once this crisis is over. Why should I help them fight? What do I stand to gain by joining this alliance?'

'You can fend off the Marathas and the nizam. You can bribe them, ambush them and force them out. The English are a different breed. I haven't seen anyone like them before. They may be less in number but they are the most dangerous.'

'I always thought the English are the greatest threat to us. If they grow any stronger, they will conquer us in no time with their deceitful ways and tactics. We need to extinguish this flame before it becomes a raging forest fire which will consume us all. But we don't have reliable allies on our side.'

'You can seek the help of the French, my lord.'

'Yes, the French would make good allies. We need to send some emissaries to them before we make any move against the English.'

'No matter what happens, we should not trust the Marathas and the nizam. If we are getting into a war with the English, we need to do so with our interests in mind. We must be prepared for a fight with the English even if we are left standing alone on the field.'

'I couldn't have put it better myself, Lutf Ali. We are in this on our own.'

The representatives of the nizam and the Marathas were informed about Hyder Ali's decision to ally with them. Pleased with his decision, they bid him farewell and went back to inform their masters. The wedding celebrations went on for a week. There was joy and laughter throughout the capital. The Savanur Pathans also bid Hyder goodbye and returned to their homes. But normalcy didn't return to Srirangapatna; Hyder Ali had ordered his army to get ready for yet another campaign.

15

1780, post monsoon, Srirangapatna

EACH ONE UNTO HIMSELF BUT THE ENEMY WAS THE SAME. The Marathas attacked the Bombay army and the nizam attacked his brother Basalat Jung and the Madras army at Guntur. Hyder was still in Srirangapatna. He was about to meet his emissaries who had just returned from Pondicherry.

'What is the response from the French?'

'They have agreed to join our campaign, my lord. They don't have a sizeable army at present but they are willing to enforce a naval blockade if you are able to do the same from land.'

'No land army?'

'General Bussy will be landing in Cuddalore soon with an army. We are on our own until then.'

'Let's make a move then. We need to seize the situation and enforce a blockade around the English capital.'

Mir Sahib, Purniah and Tipu were the new crop of generals who went with Hyder towards Madras. Lutf Ali Beg and Mohammed Ali were put in charge of the kingdom.

Unlike the last time, Hyder decided to go straight to Madras rather than conquer all the towns and forts along the way. The troops moved swiftly. The English knew the speed at which Hyder and his troops could move but they were not prepared for this rapid march. Within a few days, he had crossed the fort of Vellore, the last major fort before the English capital. There was panic in Madras. The general, Hector Munro, ordered all the troops to move out of Madras and camp in a temple at Kanchipuram. He wanted to stop Hyder before he reached Madras.

But Hyder didn't veer from his goal. He wanted to besiege Madras. He conveniently moved north, closing all paths from the north to Madras. All English troops north of Madras were blocked from reaching their capital and English reinforcements up north, especially in Guntur, now had to take a long-winded path to reach Kanchipuram – a path that could easily be intercepted by the Mysore forces.

Hyder was in his camp when the scouts arrived. 'Colonel Baillie is getting all of his troops from Guntur to join the English army at Kanchipuram. He is only a few days from meeting them.'

'We can't let that happen. Tipu, take your troops and intercept his forces. I will take my forces and block access to Kanchipuram. I don't want the English general in Kanchipuram to move forward and meet Colonel Baillie at some other place. We have him where we need them to be.'

Tipu took his troops and moved quickly out of the camp to halt Colonel Baillie's progress. Hyder moved his troops onto the road leading out of Kanchipuram to block any movement from the Kanchipuram side.

The soft spoken, middle-aged Colonel Baillie had grown up in the ranks of the Madras army, fighting Hyder Ali during his younger days and the French later. He was never harsh to his soldiers and put the welfare of his troops first. His troops in return adored him and swore unflinching loyalty to him. He was a well-loved man who had enough experience on the field to distinguish a bad decision from a good one. He knew Hector Munro had made a poor decision but he had to follow orders and march his troops from Guntur to Kanchipuram in a terrain that was prone to Mysore attacks.

Sitting in his camp, Hyder was a little surprised to see no movement from Kanchipuram. There were no scouts, no forward armies, no nothing.

Does Hector Munro really care about Colonel Baillie? Or is he a coward to step out of Kanchipuram to face me? I need to be on my guard though.

He had received information from Tipu that he had set up an ambush for Colonel Baillie and he requested his father to keep his troops ready in case he needed assistance. Something was happening on Colonel Baillie's side, but there was nothing from the general holed up in Kanchipuram. He decided that it was not for him to judge the tactical mistakes of the English.

Hyder moved his cavalry closer to the village of Polilur where Tipu had set up the ambush for the next morning. After getting some sleep, Hyder and his troops stayed vigilant the entire morning in case Tipu needed assistance. By early afternoon, cavalry scouts arrived from Polilur to Hyder's camp.

'Tipu has defeated Colonel Baillie! They have completely decimated the English army! He has taken captive more than 4,000 Europeans and 10,000 sepoys. Colonel Baillie himself has been taken captive.'

'Four thousand Europeans! This is by far the biggest victory I have achieved! The English would have never experienced such a defeat. Ask the cook to prepare sweets and distribute them. No father can be prouder than I am today. The English have just experienced the wrath of Hyder Ali.'

Hyder took his cavalry back to the main camp and waited for Tipu to arrive. By late evening, Tipu was in the camp. He said, 'Father, Colonel Baillie and his army have been vanquished. The English will now tremble at the name of Hyder Ali.'

'I am proud of your achievement, son. Tell me more about your victory.'

'They walked into my trap like lambs into a slaughterhouse. Our rockets wreaked havoc among their ranks, and their ammunition depot was blown to smithereens. They were left without ammunition. Lally, my French commander, led the cavalry attack against their square. Seeing the deaths of his soldiers, Colonel Baillie surrendered unconditionally. I have sent all of them as prisoners back to Srirangapatna.'

Meanwhile, on hearing about the defeat, the English army in Kanchipuram retreated to Madras. The noose around Madras was about to grow tighter. The French navy initiated their naval blockade of Madras and Hyder put all his troops around the capital too. 'The blockade will go on for some time now. I have enough troops to spare. I need to complete some unfinished business.'

Hyder now took his kuzzaks, musketry and artillery and moved west towards Arcot. He had a score to settle with Wallajah. The sight of cannons and Hyder Ali on the horizon was a scene right out of a nightmare for Wallajah. He immediately took his valuables, treasures and family and bolted to Madras, leaving Arcot to fend for itself. Hyder Ali, the master of many sieges, wasted no time in dismantling the defences of the fort, and soon the fort fell into the hands of the Nawab of Mysore. His thirty-year-old quest to conquer Arcot was finally complete.

As he was taking stock of the treasury, messengers arrived at his court. They said, 'The Dutch have extended their support to your campaign against the English, my lord. They are willing to hand over Tranquebar to you for a nominal payment.'

'That's good news. With Tranquebar and Dutch support, we can block the southern roads to Madras as well. Order the troops to march towards Tranquebar.'

The army started their march towards Tranquebar when reports arrived of a large convoy of supplies moving towards Madras. Purniah brought in additional news to Hyder, 'My lord, the English are sending an army to escort the supplies sent by the Thanjavur nayakas to Madras. We need to intercept these supplies before the English can reach them.'

'How is the security at Thanjavur?'

'If the English are already on the field moving to escort the convoy, then only the nayakas' soldiers must be guarding the convoy. Capturing it will be easy.

'Tipu, intercept the English while I move to take on the convoy.'

Taking a detour, Hyder's forces intercepted the convoy before the English could arrive. The haul was huge. There were enough stores and supplies to last them the entire campaign. 'With this loot, I don't need to maintain a supply chain with Srirangapatna. Any messages from Tipu? I don't see any English presence here.'

He didn't have to wait too long for an answer, as Tipu himself arrived at the camp. 'Father, I have defeated another English army. Over 3,000 Europeans and 12,000 sepoys have been imprisoned. I have also taken their commander, Colonel Braithwaite, prisoner. They have been sent to Srirangapatna in chains.'

Hyder was stunned at the prowess of his son. Tipu had achieved what no native Indian king had ever done before – he had thoroughly decimated the English. Hugging his son, Hyder said, 'Tipu, at this rate, the English will have no more men left who could fight against us. Thanjavur is badly defended right now. Go ahead and extract as much money as possible from the region. We will use the English's resources against their own forces.'

'Yes, Father. I will go to Thanjavur at once.'

With another victory under his belt, Hyder reverted to his original route to Tranquebar. As he neared the coast, he realized that the fort had been taken over by the English. Hyder wasted no time in issuing orders. 'Lay siege to the fort. Force the English out.'

Firing began in earnest, and the small garrison at the fort decided to hand it over rather than risk their lives. They exited the fort by sea, leaving the Dutch building for Hyder. Once inside the fort, the citizens informed him that these other Dutch forts had been occupied by the English too. He ordered his troops to march to these forts and capture them. The smaller garrisons in these forts also surrendered. The entire southern approach to Madras was now under Hyder's control. All that was left were some English forts in the vicinity of Madras. The end of the English in the south was near.

With troops to spare and ample resources, he got into the act of mopping up the remaining English presence outside Madras. He ordered his generals, 'Purniah, Mir Sahib, both of you fan out inside Wallajah's territory and put down all refractory palegars and any remaining English garrisons in the region. Tipu, go ahead and besiege Vellore and Ambur. I don't want any supplies from there to reach the English. I will head back to the blockade of Madras.'

The gravity of the situation was not lost on the English.

Governor General Warren Hastings was pacing up and down his office in Calcutta. The news that he received from Madras was catastrophic. He called for the Commander-in-chief of Bengal, Eyre Coote, to his office.

A frail old man with thinning hair, long nose and thick lips entered the room. He was wearing the ceremonial military dress with his shoulder strips completely full. Eyre Coote was the highest-ranking English officer in the land.

He addressed Warren Hastings, 'Good morning, sir.'

'Good morning, Sir Coote. Please have a seat. We have a situation in Madras. General Munro has made one rash decision after another, and our position in Madras is threatened. We have already lost thousands of Englishmen and the Nawab of Mysore, Hyder Ali, has closed in on Madras. The French have blockaded the port and we have no means to provide any relief. The situation is not good in Bombay either. The Marathas have hemmed our forces to a corner. Even the nizam has threatened the land corridor that connects Bengal to the Madras province. We need to do something. Or else we risk our very existence here.'

Eyre Coote was calm despite the calamitous situation. He asked, 'What do you propose we do, sir?'

'I will negotiate with the nizam to open the land corridor for our army to pass through. I understand that you have retired, but your name still carries a lot of weight in the hearts of the English soldiers and I see no diminishment in your proficiencies. Your presence in Madras will definitely boost our morale and strike fear in the hearts of our enemies. I would like you to take over the civil and military leadership at Madras.'

'Anything for the Crown, sir. I will need time to get the army and supplies ready.'

'Please do. Meanwhile, I will negotiate with the nizam for you.'

Purniah broke the bad news to Hyder in his camp. 'The Governor of Bengal, Warren Hastings, has ceded back to the nizam all of his territories that were annexed earlier. Guntur has been returned to him. Basalat Jung's claim has also been renounced by the English. They support the nizam now. In return, the English have got safe passage for General Eyre Coote and his troops through his territory. They are marching towards Madras as we speak. The nizam has withdrawn his forces back to Hyderabad.'

'Eyre Coote is here? The English are indeed in trouble. He is the best general they have. If we defeat him, the collapse of the English Empire will be imminent. I will personally intercept him.'

'What about the nizam, my lord?'

'The nizam has never been trustworthy. He has achieved his objective and he never had any intention of helping me. I always knew that. So it doesn't really matter if he has left the field. He had never been of any use to me anyway.'

Hyder called the commanders who were not actively involved in the blockade and said, 'Besiege all the English forts along the coast. Eyre Coote should not have a base in the region.'

With these orders, Hyder marched north to challenge the new general of Madras.

Eyre Coote was a seasoned general who had already made his mark in the subcontinent. He had put down the Mughals in Plassey and the French in the south. Along with Robert Clive, the two made the English the most feared force in the Indian subcontinent. Eyre Coote knew that he had a weaker hand compared to Hyder Ali. So, he stuck close to the coast during the entire march down. Hyder could only watch as Eyre Coote refused to battle and stuck to his original goal of reaching Madras as the Mysore army moved parallelly with the English forces, waiting for the Englishman to make a move into the interior.

Eyre Coote found that most of the English forts were under siege, and he had to move to the interior to make a base. Seeing no other option, he ordered his troops to move in. Hyder had been waiting for this opportunity.

'We will move the troops close to the English. We will force Coote to march towards Polilur and will ambush him at that place just as we ambushed Colonel Baillie there last year.'

As soon as Eyre Coote started moving, Hyder ordered his cannons and cavalry to attack the English troops and force them to move. Eyre Coote could do nothing but move towards Polilur. Hyder picked the same spot as Tipu for the ambush. He got his cannons and cavalry ready in the same position. But Eyre Coote was not Colonel Baillie. He saw the terrain and immediately recognized that he was being led to an ambush.

The English general ordered his men, 'Move the cannons, men! Target the field over there. Wait for my command. Scouts! Move ahead to the field. If you are attacked, retreat to your position here.'

On his orders, the cavalry scouts moved ahead. The English had minimal cavalry but Eyre Coote sent all of them ahead as bait. Hyder waited for the cavalry to enter the ambush spot. As soon as they entered the field, he screamed, 'Fire!'

Cannons burst out from all directions against the English cavalry. As ordered by Coote, they quickly retreated to cut their losses. The positions of Hyder Ali's cannons were now known to the English. He instantly ordered his artillery to target the Mysore cannons.

Cannonballs from the English side took out some of Hyder Ali's men. Hyder quickly changed his tactics. He shouted new orders, 'Change direction! Direct it towards the English!'

The cannons were slowly moved to point at their targets.

'Fire!'

It was a raging battle of cannons. The loud blasts could be heard for miles around Polilur. By evening, both sides had not been dislodged from their position. Seeing that no progress could be made, Hyder withdrew his forces. Eyre Coote too didn't see any tactical advantage in staying put at Polilur. So, he too withdrew, moving south. It was a stalemate.

Back with his commanders, Eyre Coote took a rather bold decision. 'I haven't come this far to set up base and start a long counter-attack against Hyder Ali. We have enough supplies. We will relieve and provide for every English fort besieged by the nawab. Until all the forts are replenished with supplies, we will remain on the field. We will first relieve Gingee Fort.'

The Mysore siege party at Gingee was too small to take on the entire English army. So, they retreated. Eyre Coote entered the fort, provided the garrison with necessary supplies and moved out. When the general left the fort, the Mysore party resumed their siege. This happened at every fort that was under siege in the vicinity of Madras.

Hyder was surprised by Eyre Coote's tactics. He said, 'I understand he has a lot of supplies and he keeps replenishing the forts. But how long can he do that? He will eventually run out of supplies. The sea is blocked by the French and I have blocked all the land routes. What will he do once he exhausts all stores and supplies?'

He pondered for some time.

But I am not going to wait to see what happens. I will push him to the sea. We will attack him and his supplies in transit.

The kuzzaks were ordered to attack the English and, whenever there was a chance, to steal their supplies. The Mysore musketry closely followed the cavalry to provide support fire. The English held steady despite the attacks by the Mysore army. They inflicted immense damage in return. Both sides lost a lot of men and officers in this battle. The fight went on for days and Hyder was slowly able to push Eyre Coote to the coast. Eventually, he was cornered in Porto Novo. Eyre Coote was outnumbered and was cornered by the sea on one end and Hyder Ali's troops on the other. He finally had to face the Sultan of Mysore. Eyre Coote got his troops together.

'Men, we will have to fight the nawab on the sands of Porto Novo. This is the only way we can negate the advantage he has with his cavalry and cannons. He will not be able to move either of them in the sand. It will be a straight fight between the two infantries. We need to break free from his clutches and move away from the coast.'

Hyder too knew the situation at hand and said to his generals, 'We can't take our cavalry or cannons onto the beach. It is our infantry against Coote's. We outnumber him three to one. We need to make the best use of this situation and finish him off.'

Both the infantries moved to the beach and took their positions. The longer-range and more precise muskets of the English started the firing. Hyder ordered his men to get in range. Braving the gunshots directed at them, the Mysore musketry slowly advanced towards the English. Though the Mysore infantry suffered some losses, the English infantry was in their range now, so they commenced firing. Men fell in scores on both sides. The technological superiority and doggedness of the English were matched only by the sheer numbers of the Mysore troops. The balance of the battle was slowly tilting towards Mysore, whose troops started marching for the final assault. Then, all of a sudden, cannon shots from the sea fell on the Mysore soldiers, killing a large number of them.

'The English warships have broken through the blockade! They are attacking us!'

Another cannon shot from the warship fell close to Hyder's cavalrymen, who were waiting on the sidelines. The cavalry soon moved away from the infantry. Seeing the warships come to their aid, there was a sudden boost to the morale of the English soldiers and they rushed forward to attack the Mysore soldiers. The Mysore men were no match for the rejuvenated English. Stabbed by the English bayonets, the Mysore army started thinning. Cannon shots from the warships decimated the entire rear of the Mysore musketry. Hyder knew that he would not be able to win this battle. He ordered a retreat of all his troops.

Eyre Coote didn't allow the English to pursue the retreating Mysore soldiers. Soon, Hyder's men managed to move away from the beach and were heading back to their camp.

Hyder was silent for the entire duration of the retreat and during the setting up of their camp away from Porto Novo. Scouts arrived with intelligence about Coote. Hyder was told, 'Eyre Coote has been replenished with supplies from the ships that arrived earlier. The French ships were able to drive away the English ships, but it was too late. Eyre Coote has enough supplies now. He has not set up a base again and is moving the supplies to other English forts that we have besieged.'

Hyder was lost in his own thoughts. He acknowledged the message and dismissed the scouts. He didn't issue any orders to the generals. Finally, one general asked, 'What is the next course of action, my lord?'

'I don't know. We will wait for General Bussy to arrive. Keep all the sieges active.'

Hyder had been through a lot of defeats in his life. But the defeat at Porto Novo had changed him. He didn't lose many men. He still had most of the English territory under his control but somehow, the spark in him had diminished. He did not want to pursue Eyre Coote any further. He remained in his tent for days. He was shaken out of his stupor when he received a message from his spies.

'Warren Hastings has negotiated a peace treaty with the Marathas at Salbai. The English have agreed to not recognize Raghunath Rao as the peshwa and have taken him away from the field. The Maratha campaign has ceased. Meanwhile, the Bombay army has opened a new front in Malabar.'

'I cannot lose Malabar at any cost. Send a message to Tipu to move to Malabar and finish off the English in the west. We will move to Cuddalore. General Bussy will be arriving there soon.'

Hyder was disappointed on seeing General Bussy at Cuddalore. The promised army of the French had arrived, but they were just a company of soldiers accompanying Bussy; Hyder was expecting more. This small army was not enough to finish the English hold on Madras for good. Despite the disappointment, he tried to make the best of the situation and proposed to General Bussy, 'Eyre Coote is still on the field. We need to take him out at the earliest to have any realistic chance of defeating the English.'

Bussy was reluctant to go ahead with this proposal. He said, 'We have a long campaign ahead. I would rather set up base than go after the English without any preparation.'

'Eyre Coote will definitely attack if you plan to set up a base. It is better to stay with me and fight against him on the field.'

'No, Nawab Hyder Ali. I would like to take a safer approach. I will set up a base and get ready for the campaign. If General Eyre Coote attacks, I am more than confident of defending myself.'

Hyder couldn't convince General Bussy to attack Coote. He finally said, 'All right, I must go to Arni, where my son was earlier holding a siege. I will leave some soldiers here for your protection. Do join me when you are ready.'

With these parting words, Hyder left and moved further interior to continue the siege at Arni. As Hyder had predicted, Eyre Coote mounted an attack on Bussy at Cuddalore. But the wily old Bussy was able to hold his ground and forced the English to retreat. Despite having the English on the back foot, Bussy refused to move out of Cuddalore. Eyre Coote then moved to Arni to replenish supplies at the fort.

The garrison in Arni did not yield to Hyder Ali's troops. As per the nawab's orders, there was daily firing at the fort walls. When Eyre Coote entered the field, the cannons were directed towards the relieving forces, which returned the fire. A cannon battle soon ensued.

Hyder was with his cavalry. 'Eyre Coote is not in formation. If we flank him with our cavalry, we can inflict significant damage and force them into a retreat. Move the cavalry to their flanks!'

He accompanied the cavalry to corner the English troops. Eyre Coote tried to move his infantry to cover his flanks, but by then Hyder's cavalry was already charging towards them. The wave of cavalry broke the infantry line. Eyre Coote was forced to move with his small cavalry and defend the falling flank. A hand-to-hand battle commenced between the two armies. It was a bloodbath, but one in Mysore's favour.

The fight continued for an hour. Amidst the chaos, an English soldier slashed his sword at Hyder, wounding him on his back, right next to his shoulder. Hyder, quick as ever, turned around and killed the attacker. He and his cavalry forced themselves further inside, breaking the barely complete formation of the English troops. Eyre Coote immediately called for a retreat and withdrew his forces from the field. Hyder Ali had won the day. The English forces had been pushed back.

Back in the camp that night, the hakeem had arrived to tend to the wound on Hyder's back. He gasped when he saw the wound.

'What is it, Hakeem?'

'The cut has opened up the tumour that was on your back. I think it is *surtan*, my lord.'

Hyder turned towards the hakeem. He knew cancer was incurable. Slowly, a sad smile appeared on his face.

But the hakeem didn't lose heart. He said, 'If we apply the juices from the inner lining of a lamb's stomach on the tumour, it may go away.'

Hyder said kindly to the hakeem, 'I know about surtan, Hakeem. There is no cure.'

The despairing hakeem denied it, 'No, my lord, there are medications to cure this disease. I am sure we will be able remove this tumour.'

Hyder didn't argue with his chief physician. 'Whatever you say, Hakeem.'

Despite the assurance of his hakeem, Hyder knew his time was near.

The chief physician got some French doctors to offer their opinion on the tumour as well, but it was to no avail. They didn't have a cure either. So, Hyder gave himself up to his chief physician. He ingested every medicine given to him even though he found it difficult to swallow the fluids. He lost his appetite and thus lost weight with every passing day.

He spent most of his time lying on his bed in the main tent of the camp. He looked drained, his cheeks sinking under his cheekbones and his eyes within his eye sockets. The wrinkles on his face were more pronounced now. The soldier–sultan had suddenly turned into an old man.

During his routine morning check-up with his chief physician, Hyder said, 'I am not able to sleep, Hakeem. Even though my body is decaying, my mind is not still. I have a flood of thoughts in my mind which I can't seem to control. I have acquired everything I sought and yet I feel I have nothing. I have all the power in the world and yet I feel helpless. I have never fatigued in my life and yet I feel exhausted now. I want to rest my eyes but I am not able to bring myself to sleep.'

'There is no need to worry, my lord. Everything will be alright. I will prescribe some medicine to induce some sleep. I would recommend that you eat well, my lord. A full stomach will give you good sleep.'

'I have trouble swallowing, Hakeem. I have shortness of breath. I have lost the desire for food. Give me the medicine that will make me sleep. I want to get away from all the swirling thoughts in my head.'

A few weeks later, a messenger arrived at his tent. He said, 'I have brought you some good news, my lord. The English general, Eyre Coote, passed away near Madras. The ravages of the war and age have finally taken his life.'

Hyder felt a sense of relief wash over him. 'At last, the great general has died. There is nothing on the English side to stop our progress. I can now rest in peace.'

He called in his generals for a war council. 'Continue with the siege. Send a letter to Tipu informing him about my condition. My health is deteriorating. I want to go home. My heart yearns for my wife. I want to be with my family.'

With these words, he passed on the command of the siege to his generals and started his journey back home. Carried in a palanquin, Hyder spent less time with his doctors and more with his religious advisors and even more time alone, ruminating about the future. Finally, there was a moment of clarity.

'I need to accept my fate,' he thought to himself.

There was now peace in Hyder's mind and a smile of contentment on his face. As days passed, he grew weaker and became bedridden. When he reached Chittoor, Tipu arrived to meet his ailing father.

Tipu was ushered into Hyder's camp. The hakeem left the tent, leaving the father and son alone.

A smiling but weak Hyder enquired, 'How is the situation in Malabar, Tipu?'

'We have cornered the English, Father. It's only a matter of time before we eliminate them.'

Hyder tried to get up to move closer to Tipu. But Tipu, seeing his father struggle, walked over to him and sat right next to his head.

'Son, I don't think it is prudent to take on the English. Victory against the English has come at a great cost. It's like I bought a draught of poison for one lakh gold coins. I shouldn't have taken on the English. I may conquer all the lands that belong to the English, but I will never be able to dry up the sea. The English control the seas, and we will never defeat them as long as they have supremacy over the waters. If Mysore has to survive, you will have to extend a hand of friendship to them.'

Tipu was silent. He held his father's hand as Hyder looked up at him. The Sultan of Mysore smiled for the last time and fell into a deep sleep, never to wake again.

But Tipu would not let go off his father's hand. Looking at the peaceful face of his father, he said, 'Father, I vow to never disgrace your name. I see evil in the English. I can and will never bow to them. I will never let history say that Hyder Ali's son capitulated to the treacherous English. They are an enemy like we have never seen before, and I would rather live the life of a lion for a day than that of a sheep for a hundred. I will not let you down.'

Author's Note and Acknowledgements

THE MORE I READ ABOUT HYDER ALI, THE MORE IMPROBABLE seemed the story of how he forged an empire against all odds. I got hold of archival records, over 200 years old, and scoured the pages to learn more about this remarkable figure of history. All those tales of impossible feats were true. I had to tell his story to the world, and thus begun my endeavour to write about Hyder Ali. After two years of intensive research, this book took its final form, which you hold in your hands today.

The field research conducted over these two years would not have been possible without the company of my brothers Gnaneshwar and Tejeshwar. They turned the difficult exercise of travel, search and study of remote hill forts, forgotten battefields and obscure places into an adventure as they came along with me on long road trips across multiple states in South India and kept up the spirits required for my strenuous mission.

My literary agent Anish Chandy placed his faith in this work and a newcomer like me and ensured that my story could be told to the world. I am lucky to have him as my representative.

Putting pen to paper is one thing but having the story spruced and polished is altogether another matter. I would like to thank Niyati Dhuldhoya for her efforts in editing the initial drafts and helping me get the best out of this work.

I am grateful to Teesta Guha Sarkar of Pan Macmillan India for accepting this novel. She and her team have painstakingly gone through the manuscript, helped me with edits and guided me through the entire publishing journey.

My wife Sangeetha has stood by my side through thick and thin. Her constant encouragement ensured the completion of this novel. Her conviction in my work even before it was finished kept me inspired while I wrote *Sultan* and I would, for this and many other reasons, like to dedicate this book to her.

I have tried my best to stay true to the actual historical events but the novel naturally also contains elements of fiction, serving to provide missing links and bringing more coherence to the incredible story of Hyder Ali, the great Sultan of Mysore.